OTHER BOOKS BY S.A. ISON

BLACK SOUL RISING

INOCULATION ZERO
WELCOME TO THE STONE AGE
BOOK ONE

INOCULATION ZERO
WELCOME TO THE AGE OF WAR
BOOK TWO

EMP ANTEDILUVIAN PURGE
BOOK ONE

EMP ANTEDILUVIAN FEAR

BOOK TWO

POSEIDON RUSSIAN DOOMSDAY
BOOK ONE
POSEIDON RUBBLE AND ASH
BOOK TWO

EMP PRIMEVAL

PUSHED BACK
A TIME TRAVELER'S JOURNAL
BOOK 1

**PUSHED BACK THE TIME TRAVELER'S DAUGHTERS
BOOK 2**

THE RECALCITRANT ASSASSIN

BREAKING NEWS

THE HIVE A POST-APOCALYPTIC LIFE

EMP DESOLATION

THE LONG WALK HOME

THE VERMILION STRAIN   POST-APOCALYPITIC

EXTINCTION

THE MAD DOG EVENT

DISTURBANCE IN THE WAKE

OUT OF TIME AN OLD FASHION WESTERN

FUTURE RELEASES

NO ONE'S TIME

THE INNOCUOUS MAN A.I. APOCALYPSE

For My Family

CHAPTER ONE

President Audrey sat in his favorite position at his desk: feet up, tie off, and a cigar in his teeth. He lifted his rump and ripped a fart that was likely to burn the upholstery. His watery blue eyes held malicious glee as he looked at the two men before him. A tall, mountainous man, Morty Greer and Darrel Mopes, who had the confused, wall-eyed look of a flounder. Both men sported greasy hair and unkempt beards. Neither one bright nor a brilliant moment between them, but Darrel was the smarter of the two.

"I need you boys to go door to door. We're startin' to get low on supplies. That dang Andy died with the secret location of his stash, and that, boys, was the majority of the combined stores of the town. I got a few of my boys out lookin' now, but I want more," he said, puffing like an engine. He was gratified to see both men nodding enthusiastically.

"How rough can we get?" asked Darrel, who was scratching at his beard, his dark, dirty nails rough and tatty.

"Well, I don't want you to kill 'em or nothin' like that. But you can maybe shove 'em a little and threaten. You know, that kind thing," Audrey said judiciously, his mouth puckered up in thought. He lifted his rump again and ripped out another fart. He held his cigar aloft, afraid perhaps his ass might catch fire. *Got to stop eating all those beans,* he thought.

"Sure thang, Mr. President. We'll get you what you need," Morty said, a large grin skittering across his homely face, his large teeth grimy and scummy.

"Good. Now you boys separate, start here in town and work your way out. Don't take too much, just a little from each house, that'll do it," Audrey said, a sausage-like index finger raised in emphasis. He grinned hugely, his crooked yellow teeth gleaming in the low light of his office. Both men nodded once more and left.

He sighed heavily in satisfaction. It sure was good to be president. People did what you told them, didn't argue, and, most of the time, were glad to do it. Except for Yates. His face shifted and a frown settled on his florid, heavy features. He was glad the temperature was starting to dip. It had been a hellacious summer without air conditioning. Thinking about it made him begin to sweat, and he pulled a filthy bandana from his back pocket and wiped at his face.

He let go a long stream of cigar smoke and held the stogie between his sausage fingers. He rolled it contemplatively, watching the cherry glow. Yates was starting to become a problem.

The sheriff wasn't going along with the program, and it seemed at times that he was encumbering it. He needed Yates to keep all the yahoos at bay, but Yates was giving a lot of their precious supplies away. This, in the wake of Anderson's death. They needed to find that stash, and fast. Granted, he had plenty squirreled away here at the office and at his home, but you could never have too much.

It seemed to him that he'd had to make all the hard decisions. It was good that he'd had the foresight to put some of those supplies away in the beginning. In fact, if it wasn't for him, they'd have been a day late and a dollar short when this whole thing started. Wasn't it he who'd first realized what was going on?

He'd come up with the plan to rid their town of the undesirables. Wasn't it he who'd set up the service for Gerhard's farm, so now they had produce coming in? Wasn't it his idea to put the misfits and sympathizers in the coal mine? Work them for the necessary coal? They didn't even have to feed them much.

Audrey had to think hard to find anything Yates had provided other than to act as hired gun. This would bear pondering. Perhaps after his afternoon nap. He got up and stretched, a rapid fire of small farts filling the office. He leaned over and placed his dying cigar on the ashtray. He walked over to his couch, where he'd spent many a night. The mustard-yellow couch now contoured to his bulk as he sank down into it.

8

He yawned hugely and stretched. Being an administrator and president was taxing. It had always taxed him as the mayor, but now he had his own small fiefdom to run. As he shifted his large rump on the couch, trying to find that sweet spot, he thought he might get one of those gals from the coal mine and have them come spruce up his office and his home. He yawned widely once more and fell into slumber.

XXX

It was well over a week since Clay had found the child. The whole house seemed unable to move past the child's death. It had been heartbreaking, to be so close to perhaps saving him. Yet the boy had been too far gone with starvation, his small body unable to sustain that precious spark of life. Their own children, Angela and Monroe, were thriving, however, and for that Harry was grateful. Too much suffering had already happened, and there was little to nothing he or his friends could do about it. The frustration of it hung on his shoulders like Marley's chains. He couldn't do it alone, nor with the few men that were here.

It would take a lot more people, and they all needed to plan and work together. The intel they needed was vital if they were going to rid their town of these bastards. Yet, he and his friends were far from town. A blessing, but it also stifled the process of fighting the mayor and his people. Harry knew many of the folks who lived in Beattyville, but he'd been gone so long he wasn't sure he knew them as well as he should. Telling friend from foe was vital. Any mistake in that judgement was deadly.

They hoped for a visit from Alan Tate; the teenager was long overdue. The boy was innocuous enough to travel around Beattyville unmolested. Harry looked up as Marilyn came out to the porch. She had a scarf around her hair and a smudge of dust on her cheek. He smiled at her. "Where is Monroe?"

"He's with Earl, helping him in the garden," she said grinning and then laughed, shaking her head.

"Yeah, he loves Earl and Earl loves him. Those two are darn near inseparable," Harry said and shook his head too, his eyes crinkling at the sides.

"I'm glad, though I wish he'd known his father, and his father him. But I guess Moses is watching him from heaven," she said and sighed, sitting down beside Harry on the swing.

"I almost think Monroe keeps Earl on his toes. Before all this happened, Earl's greatest excitement was at the bar in town, I think." Harry chuckled, and bumped Marilyn on her shoulder with his.

"I think it's nice they have each other. Earl is so patient with him. Children show us what's really important in life," she said.

Willene came out to the porch, a tray of sweet tea in her hands. Everyone took a glass, then she sat down in the glider.

"Just got Angela down for a nap. She's growing so fast," she said and wiped the hair out of her eyes.

"Where are Katie and Clay?" Harry asked.

"They went out on patrol together," Willene said, sipping her tea and rocking back and forth, her legs out before her.

The days were becoming crisp. Harry could feel the temperature starting to drop during the day and getting colder at night. The leaves were beginning to tinge with yellows and reds around the edges. Most days were hot; sometimes, the temperature dropped. It didn't seem like it had nearly been three months since the EMP. It was a weird combination of things going so slow yet passing quickly. Relativity, he guessed. He wondered what Einstein would think of all this. He smiled at the thought.

"Those two are getting close," Marilyn said smiling, her head rocking from side to side.

"Yes, they are. I'm not surprised. Their jobs had kept them too busy for a relationship. They have all the time in the world now," Willene said.

"I think it's nice. It feels like hope when something nice has come out of all this mess. Hope and life going on. I just wish the folks in the coal mine could be freed and the KKK put down once and for all," Marilyn said softly, her fingers tracing around the top of her glass.

"We'll get there, Marilyn. It's just going to take time getting everyone on the same page. Being so scattered, having little to no transportation is a hindrance. We're the lucky ones, though. It would take a lot of effort on the mayor's part to come out this way now. Gas, whatever is left of it, is going fast, and will be unusable in about six months. We'll have to get this settled soon. But we will, I promise," Harry said, patting her hand.

"Well, I'm sure we can put them down once we can get organized. The mayor isn't all that bright," Willene said, and raised her glass in mock salute, eliciting a laugh from Harry and Marilyn.

"Do we have any big chores that need being done?" Harry asked.

"No, not really. Most of the garden has been canned. The cabbages, pumpkins, and all that will remain until later. Earl and Monroe are getting the last of the beans and tomatoes, and a few potatoes for dinner tonight. How about the wood situation?" Willene asked.

"It's good. Boggy is out there now, checking on the downed trees. He wanted to bring in a few large chunks. He was thinking about whittling something. The wood pile is stacked. I almost don't know what to do with this idle time," Harry said.

Marilyn laughed and nudged Harry in the swing. "How about relax, Harry? There is little enough of that," she said and patted his hand.

He grinned down at her, his eyes caressing her face. He didn't know why, but she was comforting to him and made him feel peaceful. They always sat by each other on the swing now, he noticed, gravitating to each other.

He had to examine his feelings for her. He did care about her and Monroe. His thoughts drifted to Franziska Gnodtke, the woman he'd left behind in Germany. His girlfriend. He knew he'd never see her again. She was lost to him, and even now it was difficult to conjure up her face. But here beside him was a wonderful woman he'd known most of his life. He was getting to know her all over again as a woman and a mother. She was sweet and quiet, but not boring. He'd seen the ferocious mother in her when Monroe was attacked.

"What?" he asked, having missed what his sister had said.

"I said, do you think you and Earl will take another trip into town?"

"Yes. I'm thinking about going to see Wilber, Alan's grandfather. I think that, if we can coordinate with him, perhaps we can make a strike and possibly end this takeover. Get those people out of the coal mine."

"I hope Wilber can help. He's old, but he also knows a lot of people. To get those people free, my loving God, that would be wonderful," Marilyn said.

"At least the children are out of the coal mine and safe. If we can coordinate strikes in different places at the same time, we can maybe surprise the mayor's people and take them out. I've been racking my brain. If the people from the coal mine can hit their guards, say, when they are heading back for the night, that's one strike, or if we can hit the coal mine and free the people, get them away, then maybe some of them can help us. If Wilber and Boney's friends can rally, perhaps me, Clay, Boggy and Earl can join them and put the mayor and his people down once and for all. Harvesting will be over soon. This has to happen while most of the people are out of the mine."

"Remember that many of them will be extremely weak, brother. They may not be up for the fight. I'd volunteer to go with you, but I think I should stay back and help Katie and Marilyn protect this place," Willene said.

"Yes. I agree you should stay here because, should something happen, they'll need you and you will need them. I'll keep that in mind with regard to the strength of those in the mine. I'll make my plans on the assumption that there will be no help from that quarter," Harry said solemnly.

"Well, brother, you'd best plan very well. You won't get a second chance to surprise them," Willene said, and drew a long drink from her tea.

Everyone jerked at the shot that rang from the back of the house. It was too close. Harry, Willene, and Marilyn stood, listening. They looked at each other. As one, they turned, going into the house through the kitchen door.

As they came out the back door, Harry had his Glock in hand and Willene the shotgun. They walked out to the back of the large farmhouse. Up toward the back of the yard, Earl and Monroe stood in the garden, Earl's arm around the boy, a long gun in his hands. He looked down to Harry and shrugged. When Marilyn came up, Earl pushed the boy toward his mother, but Monroe clung to him.

"Sounds like it came from up there, by Boggy," Earl called, nodding toward the woods.

It wasn't uncommon these days for people to be wandering in the woods, looking for food. Harry and his friends had had several run-ins with such people, some ending up dead. Some were sent on their way, but only left with the threat of violence. Most people on the road would soon die of starvation. Harry's group was hypervigilant these days.

Harry and Earl walked toward the woods while Willene and Marilyn went back into the house with Monroe. Quietly they separated, putting thirty feet

15

between them. They listened, their eyes scanning back and forth. Harry gave Earl the hand signal to advance slowly.

Earl held his rifle up and ready, though his finger was outside the guard. Harry smiled. Earl had come a long way since the EMP. He was more confident of himself, and protective of the group. He had learned military discipline and attention to detail, both skills vital for survival. Harry's gun was up too, his eyes scanning for potential threats. He knew Boggy was out here, and Boggy had nearly been killed before.

That time, Boggy had gone fishing a little west of the property. He'd been jumped, and nearly murdered. One of the men who'd attacked Boggy had had a hand in the murder of the Santo family, Angela's parents and older brother, Robert. Thankfully Boggy had killed both men. And it had become essential to be armed in this new, violent world.

Now no one left the house without a weapon. Monroe had been taught to never touch a firearm. The household was also mindful of Angela's little hands, and either kept the weapons on them, up high, unloaded, or locked up. No one wanted a tragic accident.

Ahead, a wavering melody of whistling slipped through the forest. Harry recognized it as Boggy. His shoulders relaxed and he lowered his weapon, though he didn't holster it just yet. He looked over to Earl, who had also lowered his rifle. Walking farther and deeper into the woods, near where they had dropped trees for the next few years of firewood, they found Boggy looking down at something, whistling happily. A branch cracked under Harry's foot and Boggy's head snapped up, his dark eyes quickly locating Harry. A slow smile spread across his thin face.

"Sorry, I done forgot about that shot, shoulda come to tell ya," Boggy said grinning and wiping the sweat from his forehead with the back of his hand.

Harry holstered his gun and walked the rest of the way to see what Boggy was looking at. Earl was making his way over, though his prosthetic leg hindered him a bit in the deep brush. Rounding a low bush that had been divided by one of the falling trees, Harry found a large ten-point buck on the ground before him, a shot through its eye.

"Dang, Boggy, that's some shootin'. And that's a big 'un." Earl laughed, taking the antlers in hand and lifting the animal's head off the leafy ground. It was an impressive buck. The venison would be good cating, and good meat for the winter. Willene would can most of the meat, but Harry thought perhaps he and Earl might make some jerky too.

All three men turned when they heard someone coming through the woods to their east. Harry thought perhaps it would be Clay and Katie coming, as he and Earl had, to investigate the shot. Boggy had bagged a turkey a month or so previously. It would seem Boggy had become their hunter. Clay broke through the trees, Katie behind him. Harry saw that Clay's gun had been holstered.

A broad smile curved on Clay's face when he saw the buck. "Wow, who shot this big boy?"

"I did," Boggy said and grinned shyly.

"Damn, boy, that's some fine shooting," Clay said and patted Boggy on the shoulder with his massive hand.

"I'll head back to the house to let the girls know to expect some venison," Katie said, nodding at the men. She turned and left, leaving the four men to admire the kill.

"Should we dress it here?" Earl asked.

"Don't see why not. Let me run back to the house and get some cords and hooks from the barn and a tarp, so we can haul it back once we're finished," Clay suggested, and turned to catch up with Katie.

Earl sat on the downed tree by the carcass and pulled out his pipe. He struck a match and coaxed it to life, puffing out the fragrant smoke. Harry pulled out his pipe, scraped the bowl, and packed in fresh tobacco from a pouch he carried. He lit his and puffed a bit. His eyes crinkled against the smoke as the blue vapors wrapped around his head. He blew out and chased the cloud away.

"Well, Boggy, that's some damn fine shooting, I'll have to say," Harry said, rocking back on his heels, one hand on the pipe, the other in his pocket.

Boggy grinned and squatted by the animal, patting its large neck. His dark hand smoothed down the body to the rump. The animal had fed well, and rut would soon be upon them. The animals lost weight when that happened, as all their interest went into mating and fighting.

"I was surprised by this ol' boy. I was comin' down from yonder lot and wasn't even thinking. I seen him, and my rifle just came up, and bam, I took the shot," he said and grinned a toothy grin, his dark eyebrows waggling.

Earl laughed and shook his head, blowing out a plume of aromatic blue smoke. His face was lit up and the dentures helped to support his jawline, firming up his countenance.

"You is the luckiest hunter I know. You killed that tom turkey, now this. Dang, another one or two bucks, and we'll be set for winter," Earl sniggered.

"I reckon so," Boggy said shyly, his hand still on the grayish brown hide of the deer.

"I was thinking about going to see Wilber and Boney tomorrow. I don't want to wait until Alan comes by, not being sure when he'll show up. I've been thinking that it's coming up on harvest time and those folks from the coal mine might not get another chance to get out of there once the harvest is done," Harry announced.

"That makes sense. Yon mayor will wanna keep 'em down in that hole. It's gonna have to be a coordinated effort," Earl said, scratching his stubble chin, the rasping sound filling the forest.

"When it comes time, I wanna help. I wanna kick some of them boy's asses," Boggy said, his jaw slanted in stubborn determination.

Harry grinned and smacked Boggy on the back, then laughed. "Boggy, with your shooting skills, we'd be fools to leave you behind."

XXX

Bella May Hogg smiled at the young man. He turned to look at her in question. She grinned up at him and then nodded to the floor. She'd hit him hard on the back of the head with a rolled-up magazine.

The boy looked down and jumped back, nearly stumbling into the hutch. It was a large brown recluse spider. Bella May stepped on the arachnid, ending its life and the threat with a soft crunch. She patted the tall boy on the shoulder, smiling.

"Dang, thanks for hittin' that thing off my noggin'," Alan said, his voice just a little shaky.

"That little rascal was crawling pretty fast. I was afraid if I told you, you might try to knock it off and get bit. Those are nasty spiders."

"Yes ma'am, they is," Alan said, nodding his head vigorously.

"Go sit down son, looks like you're about to faint," she said and grinned, squeezing his thin arm. "I'll bring you some cookies."

"Yes ma'am, thank 'ya kindly."

Alan sat down on the couch and Bella May went into the kitchen. She was sure that the men below wouldn't hear anything from above, and she was certain the boy wouldn't hear them. She got a box of cookies out and then made up two glasses of lemonade from powder. It wasn't as good as homemade, but it would have to do. The days of fresh lemons were over. She sighed heavily at the thought. A lot of things were over these days. Most she wouldn't miss, but some she most certainly would.

Bringing a tray into the living room, she placed it on her coffee table. She shoved the small blue plate with cookies over to Alan, who picked one up in his large bony hand.

"Sorry they aren't homemade; those days are over. My oven is electric, though the top of it is gas."

"That's okay, missus, these is good. I can't stay long cause I gotta get that food out to others that needs it. But this is good. I was a mite hungry," he said and grinned, cookie crumbs in his teeth.

"I understand. Thank you again for thinking about me and others," she said, patting his arm. She'd not had children and had never wanted them until she was too old to have them. She'd helped mothers from time to time, especially those with newborns. That was as close as she got to having a baby in her arms. She liked this polite young man. He vaguely reminded her of someone.

"It ain't no problem. I seen the homes round here. They're all abandoned. Some smell bad too. I'm afraid to go into them."

"I reckon that many people have starved to death or may have been killed for what they had, or they might have killed themselves. This is a hard time for those who were caught unprepared. I thankfully have a small garden that is doing well."

"Yes'm, that is true enough. I have a garden me and my grandpa tend."

"Who is your grandfather?"

"Wilber Tate."

"Well I'll be. I know him. Went to school with him. He even took me to a school dance, way back when." She beamed, patting her frizzled gray hair back.

"Oh, for goodness sakes alive. I'll have ta tell him," Alan said and smiled at her, his homely face breaking open like a flower.

"He was a handsome devil back then. My name was Bella May Patterson back then."

"Are you related to Boney? And Clay, ma'am?"

"Sure, Boney is my second cousin and Clay is my third cousin. You know them?"

"Yes ma'am, I do. Some bad men tried to kill Clay. He's safe, stayin' with some friends. Boney and my grandpa is good friends. Grandpa said Boney was madder 'n a wet hen when he found out about those bad men trying to kill Clay."

Bella May's eyes narrowed, and a smile came over her lips. "So, do you know who tried to kill my cousin?"

"Grandpa said that Boney took care of him. Was one of them KKK men," Alan said, taking another cookie in his hand and dipping it into the glass of lemonade. He popped it whole into his mouth and crunched contently.

"Good for Boney. He's a good man. I knew Clay when he was a young'un. He became a policeman. We were proud of him. Hadn't seen him in a bunch of years."

"Yes ma'am. I guess I'd better be goin', got more homes to deliver to. Thank ya again, ma'am," Alan said, standing up, towering over Bella May.

"Son, do me a tremendous favor. You see any them KKK boys, say just one by himself, give him my address. I'll take care of him. Tell him that I'd pay him in food to protect me and my home," she said and smiled sweetly.

"Ma'am, he might hurt you," Alan said, a knot of worry on his forehead.

"Oh honey, don't you worry none. Old Bella May has a few tricks up her sleeve. Don't you worry none. But make sure the fella is by himself."

"Yes ma'am, I sure will."

Bella May stood and walked the boy to the door. She looked up at him and drew him in for a hug.

"Tell your grandpa Bella May says hi," she said and smiled up at him and then patted him on the shoulder.

Alan nodded, his face suffused with a pink blush of pleasure, his eyes crinkling into triangles. Bella May watched the young man get into his truck. The poor boy needed some meat on him. But Wilber had been just as skinny as the kid, way back when. She smiled at the thought of one of those bastards coming to visit her. She laughed and figured it was time to make room in the basement for company.

She grabbed a solar lantern and made her way down the dark steps into the basement. She could hear the breathing of the two men. The basement was permeated with the stink of an outhouse. She'd have to do something about that. As she came to the bottom, she lifted the lantern high. Both men turned their heads away from the bright light, their eyes squinting.

Hobo would need to be dealt with; he was down to just the two thighs. Both arms and lower legs were gone now. It would be too messy to try to harvest a thigh, so she might as well harvest the whole of him. She could can the meat for the winter. And with the man Alan sent her way, and she hoped it was a big man, she'd have enough meat to last her a while.

She went to Hobo, who still had his head turned away from her. She held the light up to his face.

"Hobo, did you want to say goodbye to Vern?" she asked.

Hobo's head turned slowly, his eyes unfocused. His beard now lay upon his chest.

"What? Where am I going?" he asked, his voice filled with confusion.

He never was that bright, Bella May thought. She shook her head, as though speaking to a child.

"I've got to make room, Hobo, and I'm afraid to say, you're out of time."

"Time for what?"

"She's gonna kill you, Hobo," Vern said in a patient voice, low and sad.

"Oh," was all Hobo said.

Sighing, Bella May looked over at Vern, smiling. "This world won't miss our poor Hobo, I'm afraid."

She thought she heard Vern say, "I will," but wasn't sure.

She bent over and pulled out the slop bucket from beneath Hobo's chair. It only had a small bit of urine in it. She'd dumped the buckets earlier that morning in one of the neighbor's back yards, some distance from her home. She'd have to use some bleach to get the smell under control. She didn't want it seeping upstairs. She knew there was a chance she could become nose deaf, and if someone were to smell it, she'd have some explaining to do. Besides, she liked a clean house. She felt inside her chicken apron's pocket and pulled out her scalpel.

"Hobo, dear, I want you to look at that far wall. Can you do that for me?" she asked.

"I sure can," he said amiably.

Holding the bucket up, she flicked the sharp blade and nicked the carotid artery along Hobo's neck, under his chin. The room filled with the tang of copper and the blood began to jet into the five-gallon bucket to mix with the urine. Hobo hadn't flinched, nor had he said a word. As the jet began to slow, he turned his head, looking over at Vern.

"Bye Vern," was all he said, and his head fell forward onto his chest. After a few minutes, Bella May was satisfied that most of the blood had vacated the body. Going over to a low cabinet, she took out gauze and went back to Hobo's body. She wrapped his neck several times, giving him a white collar.

"Why ya doing that? He's already dead," Vern asked, his voice devoid of emotion.

"I don't want to get blood all over my house, now do I? When I take him up to process him, there will be a lot of leaking. This just saves me from cleaning up the mess," Bella May explained.

She took the bucket and the solar lantern. She'd dump the blood and urine, then clean the bucket. Then she'd rig and haul the body out to the back yard and process him there. It was late afternoon, but she thought she'd have enough light to work.

Her mind was now centered on the process of butchering, and she climbed the steps of the basement. She could hear Vern's soft weeping, but thought nothing of it. There was a lot to do and she began to whistle, happy both for what Alan had delivered and for what she was about to harvest. She was looking forward to some liver and onions; it had been a while.

What luck. If that boy could get one of those KKK bastards here, I'll be set for quite a long time, she thought happily. Perhaps, once Vern was gone, she'd go out looking for another, maybe lure him in. Things were certainly looking up.

She had no neighbors; they'd all left or had died. She'd gone looking into her neighbor's homes several months back. There hadn't been much there, but she'd taken what she could find. Seeds, books, magazines and so on. The process of decay had never bothered her. It was a natural part of life.

She went back down into the basement and pulled on the ropes. She unchained the body and it fell over with a loud, hollow thump as Hobo's head bounced off the basement floor. Vern made a noise, but when Bella looked over, he was looking the other way. She stood for a moment, thinking. She'd have to wrap the rope around his neck; there was no other way to get the body up those stairs. She just hoped his head wouldn't come off in the process; that would be a pain in the ass.

CHAPTER TWO

David stood up from the table, cold fear washing down inside his body. Mary's ashen face held fear, sorrow and shock. He ran to her, scooping her up in his large arms. Jutta ran up to them, her face pale and stricken.

"Mary, are you having contractions?"

"No. I just started bleeding!"

"Is the baby moving?" Jutta asked, her voice calm, but David noticed Jutta's hands shaking.

"Yes, he's moving," Mary said, wiping at the tears with one trembling hand. She held onto David's shirt with the other.

"Take her back upstairs, David. I'll make up some red raspberry leaf tea. That will help stop the contractions if any try to start. I will also make a tea of St. John's wort; that should help keep her calm. Lay her on her left side and prop her feet up just a little," Jutta instructed, and disappeared into the kitchen.

"What am I going to do, David? It's too soon; the baby is only seven and a half months."

"I don't know much about pregnancy, but Jutta seems to. She's had five children and I think you're in good hands. The baby is still moving around and no contractions," David was nearly babbling, not

29

knowing what else to say; he didn't want her to feel the fear that was trying to suffocate him.

Mary nodded her head and laid it trustingly on his broad shoulder. His long stride ate up the distance to the second level and she pointed to the room she'd been in. He laid her in the bed and ran out to the hall. Opening a door, he saw that there were linens, towels, and blankets. Down on the bottom shelf were what looked like old sheets and beat-up rag towels. He picked several of those and took them back to Mary.

She was laying on her left side, her eyes large in her small face, fear swimming just below the surface. Gently, he slid the folded towel beneath her hips. Going to the corner of the room, where there was an old-fashioned bowl and ewer, he picked up a clean washcloth from beside it and poured water onto the washcloth. Once he'd squeezed most of it out, he walked back to the bed and sat down beside Mary. He took her small hands and held them in his large warm ones. He gently wiped the blood from her hands. Her hands were cold, and he could feel them trembling.

He squeezed them gently. "Try not to fret, Mary, I know it's hard, but try. We'll all pray hard that the baby stays safe."

"I'll try. I'm just so afraid, though," her voice trembled.

David gently moved her hair away from her face. "If you need me to stay with you, I will," he said.

"You better not David. I'd hate for you to get in trouble. You're kind of hard to miss, and if they do miss you, they'll come here looking," Mary said, her lip trembling into a smile.

He squeezed her hand gently, brought it to his lips, and kissed it.

"I'll stay until Jutta comes up with the tea. We will all be praying hard for you Mary," he said gently.

XXX

Jutta sat in a chair beside Mary's bed. It was late, she guessed near midnight. Mary was asleep. Thankfully the bleeding had stopped. The baby continued to move around, and that was good as well. She felt the small teapot; it was cool. She looked over to the other bed, where her two daughters, their lumpy forms beneath the handmade quilts, lay sound asleep, their soft snores filling the room. One slept at the foot of the bed, the other at the head. She smiled softly. They were such a big help in this difficult time. She knew it wasn't easy, and she knew they were afraid of what the future held, but they worked hard.

The world had gone topsy-turvy, and Jutta had a hard time making sense of it all. Having all the extra children meant a lot more work, but she enjoyed it; especially the children's laughter and their sweet faces. It had broken her heart when she'd first seen them, their thin faces covered in coal dust. Then Mary's frail, emaciated body. Thinking of it now brought tears to her eyes and rage in her heart. Her large hands closed into fists and her mouth thinned.

If she could but get her hands around the mayor's and the sheriff's necks, she'd squeeze the life out of them. She knew it was a futile thought, and hoped the men found a solution. There had to be some way to end this. She knew people were afraid. It was a double whammy.

First losing power with everything else, no doctors, no grocery stores, nothing. Then, when Mayor Audrey declared himself dictator and Sherriff Yates backed his play, people were undone. Those crazy men had killed innocent people, children. How could people not be afraid? Fear, cold naked fear. But the people needed courage, they needed to work together to take down these men.

Jutta sighed heavily, looking down once more at Mary's sleeping form. Her face was relaxed in sleep, and Jutta was glad. She got up heavily from the chair, her joints popping softly. She didn't think Mary would need her for a while, and one of the girls would come get her if she did. The sight of the blood had frightened her; she knew how important this baby was to Mary. It was her last link to her dead husband, Howard. Her mother, grandmother and great-grandmother had passed down the knowledge of herbs and such, mountain medicine. She had a thick journal with her family's handwritten notes of mountain and hill recipes for different ailments. She'd always used quite a few of these for her own family. Sometimes the old ways were the best ways.

Her schoolmates had laughed at her when she was a girl, calling her country and hillbilly ignorant. She imagined she had the last laugh with doctors in short supply. She had the knowledge and training from her elders and was passing it down to her girls. Some of the remedies were from her Native American connections, distant cousins, and some from her distant black cousins who'd brought their knowledge from far away Africa. Regardless of where the cures and concoctions came from, most worked very effectively. Now, more than ever, they would be very useful.

She eased into her room. Hearing her husband's soft snores, she smiled softly. The man never seemed to stop moving until he fell into bed. She changed into her nightgown and eased in. He was a heavy sleeper, and she knew she'd not wake him up. She let out a long sigh, shifting her stiff shoulders in an attempt to ease the tightness. It had been a long day and she'd be up early in the morning.

She'd heard David and her husband talking below, and then David had left with the others. They were planning to free the others in the coal mine, apparently. She knew it was dangerous and fraught with peril, but she hoped they could pull it off. They wouldn't be back for quite a few days.

Her husband rolled into her and she smiled as his hand moved about, seeking her ample hip. He sighed softly, then went back to snoring. She was his lodestone. Her hand found his and she clasped it and closed her eyes. It wasn't long before she found her slumber.

XXX

Boney and Wilber sat on Boney's porch. Both had pipes out and were puffing like steam engines. Alan had chosen the porch swing and was rocking back and forth, letting his booted feet drag the ground, making a soft shushing sound. It was peaceful and everyone was enjoying the quiet.

"I met your cousin the other day, Mr. Boney, Bella May. She said she know you, Pop Pop, when you was kids," he said.

Wilber snorted and then looked over to Boney, who rolled his eyes.

"Yeah, I knew her when she was a young'un. She was a wild one, her. Pretty too," Wilber chuckled, scratching his beard.

"She was wild. My cousin coulda had any man she wanted, but settled on that Claud feller. A spineless man I'd never wanna meet. She had that boy so twisted round her finger that the boy walked like a corkscrew," Boney said and laughed.

"That was why she married the man, 'cause he'd do what she said. She had a powerful temper, she did," Wilber said, puffing at his pipe, the blue smoke wreathing around his white hair. His knotty blue-veined hands waved the smoke from his eyes.

"She seemed real nice when I seen her. She done killed a spider that was on my head," Alan said, raising a hand to pat the back of his head.

"Yeah, my cousin is a good woman. Headstrong as all get outs, but a good woman. She seem like she doin' okay?" Boney asked.

"Yes sir, gave me cookies and lemonade. She said ta send one of them KKK fellers over to her, but I don't know," Alan said, nibbling on his lower lip.

Boney laughed and slapped his knee. His eyes wrinkled up in a huge grin, nearly disappearing into his creased face.

"You send on one of them booger-eaters to her. She'll take care of that bastard but good. She don't look it, but she is a strong woman. And crafty as

35

hell. She'll take care of him in a skinny minute. One less bastard we got to worry for."

Wilber nodded. "That's so. I never seen a stronger woman. Freakishly strong. Give her a bat or board, she'd have that feller subdued in no time. Then she'd go plant him in her garden," he said and sniggered, his face glowing red.

Alan grinned and sat back, the worried frown leaving his face. He stared out into the distance, sipping his warm sun tea. The sun was starting to head over the horizon, and the wind was cooling.

"So, when do we go out next?" Wilber asked, his eyes searching Boney.

"I've been thinking, especially since we have the names of them KKK fellers."

Before Boney could expand, they heard the sound of a truck. Everyone sat forward, Boney checking the .45 tucked in the small of his back. They waited for the truck to come near. Alan was the first to recognize the occupants of the truck.

"It's Harry, Earl, and Clay, Pop Pop!" he said excitedly.

"Clay?" Boney said, a smile stretching out the wrinkles on his old face. He stood up, waiting for the truck to pull to a stop. He watched as the men got out of the old truck, and his eyes curved over his cousin's face, happy to see him. Clay stepped up to the porch and engulfed his shorter cousin in a bear hug.

The old man cackled and slapped the younger man on his large and broad back.

"You're a sight fir sore eyes, young'un."

"You too, Boney. I'm glad to see you and that you're doing well," Clay said and grinned down at the old man. Alan scooted over, making space for Harry and Clay. Harry stepped over to shake Boney's hand.

"Harry Banks, and this is Earl Bayheart."

"Good ta meet ya, son," Boney said to Harry. "I knew your grandpa. Good man. Sorry to hear he passed on. Good to meet you as well, Earl," Boney said, smiling. Earl nodded and shook his hand.

"Thank you, sir. I've heard about some of your exploits with our common problem," Harry said.

"Shoot." Boney laughed and waved it away. "That was some kinda fun, boy. We sure did enjoy it. We was just talkin' about your cousin, Bella May," he said to Clay. "You ever meet her?"

"Yes, sir, I sure did," he said. "Good woman. I heard that back, after the Korean war, she helped widows and their children with growing food. She was a nurse and saw to their care."

"Yeah. She meant a lot to those who ain't had much. She's a hard woman and irascible, but she got a good heart. She wanted Alan here to send her a KKK feller so she could show him the right of things," he said and tittered.

37

Clay and Harry both raised their eyebrows at that. Earl snorted.

"Don't fret. She'll take care of that gomer and there'll be one less we got ta worry for," Boney said with a hint of a smile.

"Earl, Clay, and I came to speak with you both. We hope to maybe work out some kind of plan. I think that the opportunity for getting the folks from the coal mine ends with the end of harvest. Once the harvest is done, there will be no excuses for the people to get out of the mine," Harry said, pulling out his pipe to light it.

"That does bear thinkin' about. I've come across some intel about some members of their organization," Boney said and smiled grimly.

"Have you now? Very interesting. How many people are we looking at?" Harry asked, sitting back and balancing his boot on his knee.

"Well now, that'd be about eight, not counting the sheriff and his three deputies, Grady, Learn, and Smalls. Also, Mayor Peckerwood and his civilian bodyguards. But they're untrained, so I'm sure they'd scatter once things got hot," Boney said, his grey bushy eyebrows bouncing up and down above his eyes.

"Reckon if me and Boney take out a couple of them gomers, that'd be a couple less. Not sure how many is guardin' the coal mine. We might need to get some small arms over ta the farm, give 'em to the folks heading back to the mine," Wilber suggested.

"Sounds good. Maybe we can coordinate to hit all targets at once. I was thinking do a first strike at the coal mine. It would need to be late afternoon. Maybe once the bus returns with the folks, back to the coal mine. As they off-load, position me, you, and a couple others hidden to take out any that the hostages can't take out on their own. Or take the guards out before the bus gets back to the coal mine," Harry suggested. Earl and Clay nodded their agreement.

Boney puffed on his pipe, thinking. He rocked back and forth, his booted foot tapping the floorboards of the porch. He nodded a few times and grunted. His mouth worked along the pipe stem, puffing. Finally, he squinted up at Harry and smiled.

"Sounds like a good plan. Me, you, Clay, and Wilber can head over early, get set up. As far as I know, there are only two to four guards at any one time there, plus the two that ride the bus with the hostages. Also, the driver. But from what I heard, the guards that are on the bus are on our side," Boney said.

"Then, really, we don't need to worry about getting small arms to the hostages. Maybe get them some, just in case, but I think between the four of us, we can take the guards out," Harry said, a broad smile crossing his face.

"That'd be 'bout right. Unless something goes really wrong, should be easy. Pick our targets and put 'em into the dirt," Wilber said.

"What then?" Alan asked, and all eyes turned to him.

"Then we get all them folks out of the coal mine. Bring them up and use the bus to take them out of there," Earl said.

"Take 'em to where? Do they even got homes to go home to?" Alan worried.

"That's a thought. And those folks ain't gonna be the strongest, so they can't fight," Wilber said.

"Let me ponder on that for a bit. See what I can come up with," Boney said.

"Once that's figured out, then I think we should head out and hit the rest of the targets at once, or within a short span of time. This is where we will need intel. Maybe leave some of the guards alive to question," Harry said.

"Me and my grandson can ask around, covert-like. Get a feel to see where most of them idgits linger. We already know where Audrey and Yates live. They'll either be at the courthouse or home, I'd imagine," Wilber said.

"I want to take out Yates. I owe that sorry bastard," Clay said, his mouth flat with suppressed rage, his eyes narrowed and his eyes like hard brown stones. "Whoever takes out Audrey will also need to take out his bodyguards."

"I have Earl and Boggy, who is a damn fine shot. They'll be coming with us," Harry said, and Earl grinned, his face flushing.

"So that is six, plus two or three from the coal mine, and we got the Edison twins and Sherman Collins, but he's Navy," Boney said, and winked at Clay, who grinned back.

"Yeah, an' we got Hoover. Just wish we had Thornton, rest his soul," Wilber said sadly.

"You got me too, Pop Pop. I wanna help too. I'm a good shot," Alan said, his narrow chest puffing out.

Boney bit his bottom lip, trying not to laugh at the boy. He was the spit of his grandfather at that age.

All eyes looked at Wilber, who sat silent for a few minutes. Alan chewed on a nail as he waited to hear what his grandfather had to say.

"Well, the young'un has seen a lot and been through a lot. He's damn near a man, I reckon. Yeah, boy, you can go, but you'll stay to the rear. Make sure you watch our six."

The rest of the afternoon was spent talking tactics and strategies. It would be difficult to hit multiple targets at the same time, but they couldn't afford to let any of the KKK members slip the net;

they'd only come back later. That wouldn't be good.

It was getting close to evening when the meeting broke up. Boney waved farewell to his cousin. He was glad to see that Clay had survived the initial cull. And that was what it was, culling. The mayor and sheriff had culled folks they didn't want in their new world.

Boney sat on the porch, rocking quietly. He could hear the night birds begin their chorus. Somewhere in the distance, he heard the soft call of the whippoorwill.

He sure missed Thornton Sherman. His heart still felt bruised over the murder and ill-treatment of the Marine. He knew his cousin wanted Yates, but he might as well help out a bit on that front. Also, he thought he might pay Grady an impromptu visit one night. Take that little shit out in a leisurely fashion, just as the bastard had done to his friend Thornton.

XXX

"I think I need a house servant," Audrey said, his feet propped up on his desk.

He was smoking one of the last of his cigars. He'd asked Yates for some of his, but Danny wasn't going to give over his stash; they'd be the last cigars he'd ever get and he wasn't giving them away to this pissant. Audrey had done nothing but sit on his

42

fat ass, bitching and complaining about every move Yates and his men made.

"What in the hell? Why?" Danny Yates asked. "You spend most of your time here, Rupert,"

"Well, my place is getting kinda ripe, I guess you could say. Need someone to come spruce it up."

"Why don't you just hire one of the ladies around town? I'm sure they'd work cheap, maybe food, fuel?" Yates suggested.

"Naw, I ain't payin' for that. I was thinking on getting that black snooty bitch, Mary Lou Jaspers. I want to see her cleaning my house," Audrey said, smiling a big yellow toothy smile.

"We have bigger problems than your house getting clean, for Christ sakes. We have a town to keep safe and people to keep in line. Anderson is dead, Smalls is missing, presumed dead, no one's seen hide nor hair of him. Winter's coming and, though we got coal, our food stocks are going down. Anderson was the only one who knew the location of the bulk of the food. We need to send our people out looking for that food or we're gonna have problems this winter," Yates said.

"So, get men and go look. Why do I have to think up the solution for everything? There are enough peckerwoods around you shouldn't have to worry about bodies."

"Rupert, I need men we can trust. That number is dwindling as the days go on. I'll be pairing up our boys with some of the local civilians. We need to find Anderson's stash."

Audrey flipped his hand in dismissal. "Fine. Do what needs doing. Take care of it."

Yates stood, his blue eyes boring down at the mayor, who was puffing away at his cigar. *Little goddamn turd is what he is,* Yates thought darkly. *He needs to be flushed away.*

He left the office, passing the three men who sat around the outer chamber picking their noses. Useless to a man. Just like Audrey. He was busting his ass to keep them solvent in food, weapons, and people. Sooner or later, he was going to have to deal with the mayor, but he needed to get his men out there looking for that food stash.

Yates exited the building and walked over to the precinct building, a block up the street. He took note of several civilians lingering around the steps. He didn't think they looked dangerous, but one could never be too careful these days. As he drew closer, he could see their thin faces.

"Sheriff… I mean, vice president, my wife and kids are starving. Is there any food to be had?" a tall, thin man asked. He looked to be in his forties, his face weathered and hard.

Yates lifted his hand to stop the others from surrounding him. They all looked bad. "It's just

44

sheriff, and I'm trying to locate some supplies. One of our people, who knew the supply's location, has passed away. Unfortunately, we don't know where that is. I'm having my men locate it as we speak. Did you folks plant gardens?" he asked, looking around at the faces bobbing around him.

"Well, no. We figured the government would make sure we got what we needed. We knew it might take a while, but, well, you know, they should be taking care of us," the thin man whined.

Yates's lip curled and he shook his head.

"So, you've been sitting on your ass this whole time? You've not planted gardens? I suggest you go and see what you can hunt and catch for your family. See about starting some beans and squash or it's gonna be a hard winter. The government isn't coming. If they've not come by now, I don't see them coming any time soon."

The faces around him turned bright red, whether from shame or rage he couldn't tell, and he really didn't give a shit. He had too much on his plate with a useless mayor and people going missing and getting killed. He was glad his own wife had planted a garden, but he sure as hell wasn't going to tell these people.

"Well, you're the government; why ain't you helping us," the thin man said belligerently.

"No, I'm the law. Why don't you go and talk to the mayor? *He* is the government!" Yates snarled.

He turned and headed into the building, slamming the door behind him. He could still hear the grumbling outside.

Walking into the large room, he saw Officer Tom Learn sitting back in a chair, a cigarette hanging off his lip as he read a magazine.

"Tom, go find Grady, Archer, Tweet, and Finch. Tell them to each double up with a civilian; then get your asses out there and locate Anderson's hoard. We're gonna be facing a shit storm if we don't locate those supplies soon."

"Sure thing, Sheriff. I take it the mayor wasn't any help?" Officer Learn said, nodding and stood, tossing the magazine onto the chair.

"That asshole couldn't find his shit in a shoebox. If you can find men you can trust, the more the better," Yates said, and went to his office. He needed a drink, and he had a bottle of Jack in his desk drawer.

XXX

Morty Greer walked down the sidewalk, a basket of apples under his arm. He'd helped himself to an apple tree that one of the townspeople had in their yard. Some of the apples weren't quite ripe, but they were sweet, if a little tart. The owner didn't have much in the way of food. He'd gotten a can of beans and a box of pasta.

46

Morty put it in the back of his truck. Then he leaned against the truck, looking up and down the street. It was quiet. Quiet always made him nervous. His dung-colored eyes shifted around, looking into windows of the houses that lined this street.

It hadn't been going well. Most of the people he'd confronted had very little. At first, he'd not believed them and had rifled through their cupboards and pantries. He'd even gone down into their basements. He'd even smacked one man around. Nothing. Morty looked at his knuckles and saw dried blood. He spat on his hand and then wiped it on his pant leg.

He hated to disappoint the president, but at least he had the apples and a few cans of food. He let out a heavy sigh and stood erect as he walked to the next house down the line. He knew Darrel was elsewhere, doing the same thing. Darrel had suggested they keep a little of the supplies for themselves. Morty thought that was a good idea, so he'd set aside a couple of cans.

He scratched his rump as he walked, his head turning and watching for activity up and down the empty street. He took note of a house that might have prospects.

He went up the walkway and raised a big hand and pounded on the door. He cocked his head sideways, listening. He hammered again and was just about to turn the doorknob when the door

47

swung open. Two women stood at the door, one young, about twenty, he thought, and the other older, he figured her mother.

He grinned. "Ladies. The president done sent me out to gather supplies. You need to give over some of what you got."

"We ain't got much, mister. We can barely feed ourselves," the older woman said.

He could see fear in her eyes and he grinned. "Well, sorry, but that ain't no excuse. I got to come in and see what y'all got," he said, and pushed past both women easily. He walked into the dim kitchen beyond. The only window stood over the sink. He looked around the neat home. There were pictures of the family.

"Where's your man?" he asked.

"He was in Lexington when everything went ta hell," the older woman answered. Morty saw that she held her daughter behind her. Both were plain and had thin, hard faces.

Morty grunted and began opening cabinets. He saw cans of soups and canned meats. He looked over his shoulders. The older woman looked angry and afraid. His eyes went to her daughter, and the woman turned and whispered something. The daughter left; his eyes followed her.

"She kin be yours, but you can't take none of our food," the woman said, her mouth a flat line that slashed across her face. She folded her arms across her narrow chest.

Morty licked his lips and turned back to the cabinet, looking at the numerous cans. Then he looked back at the woman. "She ain't gonna scream or nothin' is she?"

"Naw, but don't you rough her up none. And if you want more of her, you gotta bring food next time," the woman said, nodding her head to the cabinet.

"What?" Morty said, uncomprehending.

The woman huffed, exasperated. She stared at him. When he didn't catch on, she said, "If you want any more visits with her, you got to bring some food with you to pay for it. We ain't given it for free. You got to pay for layin' with her. You got to pay with food."

"Oh. Alright," Morty said, and left the house, going out to the truck, his feet moving faster than they had in a long time.

He bent over the truck bed, pulled out a box of pasta, and went back into the house. He handed the box over to the surprised woman and went into the back of the house in search of the younger woman. There was a huge grin on the man's face.

CHAPTER THREE

David Colman, Gideon Elliot, and Steven Stroh sat around a solitary candle, its sputtering light casting jittery shadows. Without the children, it was quiet. The sound of a woman weeping could be heard from time to time, but that was normal. At some point or other, everyone in the coal mine had wept. The cold was beginning to creep down into the cavern. David didn't want to think what winter would be like.

He worried for Mary and hoped she still had the baby. He'd had to leave, otherwise it would have brought the guards to the Friedhof farm and they would have taken Mary. Then she'd have lost the baby for sure. Also, then Gerhard and his family would be in this hole along with everyone else. He shuddered at the thought.

"We'll have to move fast once we get notice of a go. There won't be much planning to get out of here. I'm hoping Gerhard is taking care of that. The two guards and the driver are on board as well. We may only have short notice, so keep that in mind," David said.

The other men had been out to the farm once or twice, but both were thin now, as was everyone else in the mine. The hostages were now thoroughly

50

searched for food on return, so they no longer brought any back.

"How do you think Mary's doing?" Gideon asked.

"Jutta has been taking good care of her since she arrived at the farm. She's put on a good amount of weight, which is very good for her and the baby. If anyone can save the baby, it's Jutta," David said, hope lacing his voice.

"I'd love to get my hands on that bastard, Yates," Steven said, then he coughed and wiped at his mouth. They'd taken him to the farm a few times, knowing he needed the fresh air.

David was afraid he was developing lung problems. Black lung was sometimes a byproduct of working in the mines. Many miners had died over the years from the ailment. David's own grandfather had. He remembered, as a youth, his grandfather coming home, coated with the dust.

His grandfather would walk into the home, dark blue overalls patched up from tears and burns. He wore a banged-up silver hardhat, and a light that sat in front like a cyclops. He had his black metal lunch bucket that fit neatly under his arm. The man had seemed like a giant to David, but now, looking back, his grandfather had shrunk to nearly nothing from the black lung.

Each of them had masks or bandanas covering their faces, but when they ate, they felt the coal dust in their mouths, the grit a constant companion. He looked forward to the day when they could get out.

"What will you do once you're free of this place?" Stroh asked both men, wiping his face with a filthy handkerchief. It simply moved the grime from one side of his face to the other.

"Take a damn bath in the river. I don't care if it is freezing. I want this grit off me." Gideon laughed, and the other men joined in. Then he sighed heavily, shaking his head. "I'll see if our house is still standing, but even if it is, it won't be fit to live in. I'll see what I can take from that. Head into the mountains. Then start huntin'. I gotta get my boys fed, keep my family whole,"

"Same here. I'm glad Jutta and Gerhard are giving us some food. That will help us a lot until we can plant next year," Steven added.

"I live in an apartment, but I might just look for an abandoned house. That way, I'll have a bit of land to plant a garden on, come next spring," David said. He didn't add that he hoped that Mary and her child would eventually come live with him. That was his secret dream.

"Do you suppose there are many people left out there?" Gideon asked.

"Don't know. Might not be, with the mayor and sheriff stealing everything. I think maybe the folks farther out of town are faring better. Anyone in town is a target for their thievery," Steven said. His mouth turned down, grooves biting deep into his skin.

"Yeah, I'd say that's about right. Those in the hills and mountains stand a better chance of staying out of their crosshairs," David agreed.

"My grandparents had land up in the mountains. After all this is over, I think, after we go home and see what is what, I might just take my family there. It isn't far from here, and it has a wood stove to cook and heat the old homestead, and it has a good well on it. My folks were going to renovate it, and even started on some of it. But after a couple of winters, they decided to head down to Florida. I think I'll get what I can from our home and head there," Gideon said thoughtfully.

"That sounds really nice. I wish me and Ginna could take Robert to some place like that," Stroh said wistfully.

David smiled, Robert had been one of the first children to leave the coal mine, the four-year-old going with Jack, a five-year-old. He couldn't blame them; he wanted away from this place.

"Steven, you and Ginna would be more than welcome to come with us. There's plenty of room, and I'd feel better having another man around to help guard it. Plus, you're a damn fine shot, and that'll come in handy hunting," Gideon offered softly.

Stroh's eyes grew enormous, and then the sheen of tears filled his eyes. He and his wife lived in a small apartment with their son. Going back to that small place wasn't an option, as there was no land to grow a garden, nothing for food preparation, and no water source. He'd told them how the little apartment fit them well, but like most places, it wasn't suited for off-grid living, as David knew very well.

"You sure, Gideon? You'd better ask Julie. She might have something to say about that," he said, though hope burned bright in his eyes, David could see.

"Heck yeah. Julie and I've been talking about when we get out of here. As I said, we'd thought to go back to our house, but she pointed out we had no running water, so no toilets. She'd reminded me, in fact, about the old homestead. It has an outhouse, hand pump, well, and sits high in the mountains with a good view of the valley. It will take some fixing up, but if you don't mind working hard, you and your family are welcome," Gideon said.

Steven stood up and stepped over to Gideon. Though Steve was the smaller man, he damned near picked Gideon up in a bear hug.

David felt his eyes prickle with tears. It made his heart swell. People were trying to help one another, just as it should be. He was glad for both

54

men. He'd have to see about his own home, but that
was fine. It was important to get it right.

XXX

Morty Greer was looking through the pantry of
a modest little home. The family stood by, their
faces pointing down to the ground in fear. Morty
was a big man and had big appetites. Both Yates
and Audrey had given him and his comrades free
reign to forage for supplies. After all, the
brotherhood needed food and supplies to ensure
their continuance.

Audrey had impressed upon Morty the fact that
their group had important work to do. It was every
citizen's duty to supply the government with food
and supplies. How else could it run the town? Morty
didn't know about all that, but when he was told to
do something, he did it. He was good that way.

"Now y'all ain't holding out on me, is you?" he
asked over his shoulder as he was digging around.
There wasn't a whole hell of a lot here.

"No, sir, that's all we got," the slender young
man said, his arm protectively around his wife and
ten-year-old daughter.

"Well shit, you ain't got a pot ta piss in," Morty
huffed and backed out of the pantry. He looked at
the little family, scrutinizing them closely. They
didn't have an ounce of fat on them, unlike himself.

He scratched at his large belly, his dirty nails leaving a trail of grime on his shirt.

"If I find out you're holding out, I'll burn this place down with you in it," he growled and went to the door.

Stepping out of the house, he saw a thin young man walking down the street. He started toward him, hitching his pants up. He walked toward the young man and began following him.

"Hey you, stop," he called.

The young man looked around and then at him, his eyebrows raised in question. He stopped and waited for Morty to come abreast.

"Where you live?" he asked the young man.

"I live over on Cumberland Street."

"Why is you over here?" Morty questioned.

"I was lookin' for someone to help. I got a friend, she needs protecting. I was tryin' to see if I could find someone to help her. She said she'd pay in food and shelter."

"So why don't you help her?" Morty asked, surprised.

"I can't. My grandpa is in a bad way; he needs me ta be with him and take care of him," the young man said, his homely face sorrowful.

"Oh, okay. Sorry for your grandpa. So where does this gal live?"

"She lives in Blue Jay Estates, over on Calgary Lane. Her house number is twenty-three. Her name is Bella May. She's a nice lady," the young man said and grinned a toothy grin.

Morty grinned as well, and asked, "She got a lot of food then?"

"I ain't sure, no more than most, maybe, but she's alone an old. I think she's just afraid. I wished I could help her, but I can't, I gotta help my grandpa," the young man said, his hands now in his back pockets.

"Okay, move along then." Morty jerked a fat thumb over his shoulder. He walked over to his beat-down Ford truck and climbed in. He took a last look around the neighborhood. It had been a bust here, and a colossal waste of his time. He knew where Blue Jay Estates was, and he grinned to himself. He'd just take a little drive over and see what was what.

An old lady would be easy pickings, and he could maybe hold up for a few days before he took the rest of the food in. If there was any food left, he chuckled. He could also use some of it to go visit that sweet little gal. He sure did like her; not her mom so much, but she was nice and didn't smell half bad.

It only took a matter of ten minutes and he'd arrived at the Blue Jay Estates. The place was a shambles. The yards were overgrown and trash blew around in swirls in the street. Houses looked vacated, doors kicked in, windows broken.

It reminded Morty of a ghost town and sent a shiver down his back. Some houses had the contents scattered about the yard, as though they'd vomited it out. He wondered where the people had gone. The hair rose on his arms and he shivered again. He didn't know why this place bothered him. Maybe he'd just take what he could take from the old gal and skedaddle.

Things sure went to shit fast, he thought.

He found the street and then the house. It too had an overgrown yard. He saw the gnomes, and grinned. Around him, the other homes had the abandoned feel and look. *I guess I'd be afraid too, if I lived here. Ain't nobody around*, he thought, and shivered. He raked his dirty nails through his hair, the uncomfortable prickle irritating him.

He got out of his truck and slammed the door. Hitching up his pants, he walked up the sidewalk to the house. He'd have walked right in the door, but he wanted to at least act like he was here to help. *Until I don't*, he laughed to himself. He lifted a hand and knocked loud and hard on Bella May's door, a broad smile on his face.

XXX

Wilber had the truck today; he'd told Alan that he needed to see Gerhard Friedhof. As he drove down the deserted highway, a frisson of sadness and satisfaction went through him. He was glad there were no other vehicles on the road; he'd not have to worry about coming across someone who wanted whatever he had on him. But he was sad that it had come to this. The world had gotten a whole lot smaller.

He saw the farm ahead and got off the road and onto the long drive. Dirt flew up behind him and he could hear the rocks pinging beneath his truck. Alan had become adept at siphoning gas from abandoned vehicles. He knew that day would come to an end as the gas either deteriorated beyond use or ran out completely.

He saw one of the farmhands heading to the main house and slowed down. He didn't want to get shot at, in case they'd had trouble in the past. Pulling his truck into the dooryard, he saw Gerhard come out, Jutta behind. He smiled and raised his hand in greeting. Gerhard grinned and lifted his hand.

"Howdy Gerhard, how ya been?"

"Ah, fair to middlin', you?"

"Fine as a frog's hair." Wilber laughed, reached out, and shook Gerhard's hand. He nodded to Jutta, and she blushed prettily and went back into the house.

"What brings you out our way, Wilber?"

"Me an' my friends have been talkin'. Time is running out for them folks in the mine. I want to pass along, we want to set up some kinda ambush,"

59

Wilber said, walking alongside Gerhard as they stepped into an empty field. Wilber looked around. The field had been picked clean. He looked over to a corn field, still green and lush. It filled his heart with hope.

"The people from the mine that come here, they been talkin' too. We need small arms to sneak into the mine," Gerhard said.

"We was thinking about that and about getting them out the next time they're here. When will that be?"

"Week after next. They come to help with the corn in yonder field," he said, nodding toward the corn field.

"My people will be at the mine on the afternoon those people head back to the coal mine. Do you know how many guards are at the coal mine?" Wilber asked.

"David said there are normally two guards outside the mine whenever they return from here. The two guards that accompany the bus are on our side, as is the driver."

"That's good. We thought that was the case. We can have our men take the guards out when the bus goes back. Then we get the folks out of the coal mine. We'll need to find places for them to stay until we've taken out Yates's men, and Audrey's people as well. We think we know most of the gomers that need killing. Boney has a list of names and we figure once we take out the main body of the KKK, the rest will either disappear or convert," Wilber said, taking out his pipe and lighting it.

"Can you tell 'em when they come that morning. We'll see about getting arms. We also need volunteers to help us fight, those who are fit and strong enough," Wilber continued.

"I'll let 'em know. I can fight," Gerhard said.

"No. You have a big family and one hell of a lot of responsibilities. You're one of the few big farmers left. Our town needs you and yours to stay here and keep doin' what you're doin'. But thank you kindly. We'll need to also figure out where to put all the folks that come out of the mine. Put on your thinking cap and think on where they kin all go. We'll be thinking as well," Wilber said, heading back to his truck.

"You think we can do this Wilber? Take back our town?"

"Yes, I do. We have a lot of fine people who are trapped under Audrey's thumb, who are intimidated by Yates's goons. We need to all have a little courage, a little faith. Once we break the KKK's back, we can take our town back. Once we take our town back, I think people will want to work together. I'm also thinkin' that, after living the way they have been, the good people of Beattyville will want a better life, a better way of working together to make not only their own lives better, but

61

that of the community as well. Something honest and something everyone can live with." He winked, his face nearly caving in from the gesture.

"I sure do hope so. I want my children to grow up free. Free from fear and acrimony," Gerhard said, his hands moving about him, ceaseless.

Wilber smiled. The man rarely stayed still. "That's what we want for all our babies." Wilber thought of Alan.

XXX

Bella May looked out the peephole, and grinned when she saw a large man outside her door. Looking behind her, she checked that everything was ready. She opened the door, hunching her shoulders and softening her face. She didn't want to look too strong; she needed to look helpless.

"Yes?" she said, her voice quavering, unfocused and foggy.

The man before her grinned broadly. She smirked to herself. He was a big one. She opened the door and let him enter.

"I was told you need a little protection," he said.

She watched him as he looked around her home, his behavior reminding her of a predator. Her smile grew. "Why yes. Did that young man send you here?"

"Yes. How can I help?"

"Well, I'd like for you to stay here. I have some food in the basement I need brought up. Do you think you could help me? You look big and strong," she said and watched carefully as his grin widened.

"Sure. Where's your basement?"

"Over here dear," she said, and pointed to the basement door.

He passed her and went to the door, as he opened it, she reached for the baseball bat. When the door was opened, she swung the bat and cracked him on the back of his big head. There was a hollow *whump*. The man had thick hair and she hoped she'd hit him hard enough.

He didn't make a sound as he crumpled boneless to the floor and rolled down the steps into the basement. It was a slow process, his big body hitting the basement walls as he went down. She thought she might have to go and kick him the rest of the way, but he eventually made it to the bottom. She let out a satisfied sigh, and smiled. Going to the kitchen, she got her solar lantern.

She made her way down the steps and stepped over the large body. She hummed as she set her lantern on her work table. She could feel Vern's eyes drilling into her back.

"Yes, Vern, what is it?"

"You got him. Can you let me go? I swear, I won't tell a soul."

"Vern, you have no arms and no feet. What are you going to do out there?"

"I can live," Vern said softly.

"That would just be cruel. You at least have a stay of execution, Vern. I have this large man here. Looks like he will last me a long time. You can relax and enjoy the extended time."

Bella May moved about the basement, pulling nylon ropes between the downed man and the pullies. She cut the clothing off the large man, throwing it into a pile to burn later. It took a bit of doing, but finally she got the unconscious man hoisted into the chair. She secured him, adding a few more loops of chain. He was a big man and it wouldn't do for him to break free. She also put a chain around his neck, just in case he worked himself loose.

She'd been doing this for too long to screw it up by underestimating a man. She then checked his wound and was satisfied. She'd not broken the skin, but there was a good size lump in the back of his head. She went upstairs to retrieve a bucket of water and a rag. Taking the rag, she began to wash him. She wrinkled her nose.

"I'll swear, some of these men just plain stink. I don't understand the aversion to simple soap and water. It doesn't take that much water to keep your body clean," she grumped.

"Did you kill him?" Vern asked, no emotion evident.

"Naw, didn't even break the skin. You have to finesse these things. Yes sir, this is a nice big boy. Good eatin'," she said and tittered, smacking the rounded hairy belly.

A long, low moan came, and his eyes began to flutter open. She smiled and looked into his eyes. She enjoyed these first few moments, when their confusion cleared to awareness, and then to reality and clarity. There was power, and it was almost as good as the food she took.

"What ... what ... oh shit, my head hurts. What happened?" the man groaned.

"Hello, young man. What is your name?" Bella May asked, her voice kind and encouraging.

"What? My, my name's Morty," he said, blinking hard, trying to focus on her.

"Hey Morty," Vern called in a dead voice.

"Vern?" Morty asked, trying to locate the voice in the room. His eyes squinted and couldn't seem to focus.

Bella May watched the two men. This was better than TV. Morty was turning his head, eyes blinking rapidly. He tried to lean forward but was unable to. He didn't quite understand why.

"Vern? Why are you neked?" Morty asked, confused.

"Sorry Morty, you've been caught."

"What do ya mean, *caught*?" he asked, wincing as he shook his head.

"He means that you stepped into the wrong house, young man," Bella May said.

Morty tracked her voice and found her in her position by the table. He still looked confused. He looked back to Vern, then his eyes bulged. Bella May figured he'd just noticed Vern was missing arms and feet.

"Jesus Christ, Vern, what happened to you? Where are your arms? And your feet? Christ!" Morty expostulated.

"Bella May ate my arms and my feet, Morty. You're next," Vern said, his voice low.

Bella May saw the fear as it entered Morty's eyes, as he looked over to her, then for the first time realized he too was secured and also naked. She watched as his eyes grew enormous, then sheened with unshed tears. His eyes went back to Vern. His lips trembled and he began to shake his head. His body began to rock, but the chains held him secure and tight to the metal support. The sound of the metal chains clinked against the support, the chime of a trap. His teeth gritted as he struggled against his bonds futilely.

Then he screamed, "Nooooooooooooooooo!"

Bella May smiled.

XXX

Mary was confined to the bed, sipping her milked-down coffee as Jutta sat beside her. There was a TV tray between them, holding a plate of biscuits, coffee gravy, sliced tomatoes, and two eggs over easy. She wasn't very hungry, but Jutta refused to leave until she ate. She hoped the coffee would help bring up her appetite. Luckily, she'd had no more bleeding, and between meals she drank the teas Jutta and her daughters brought to her.

Beside her on the bed were stacks of books and a deck of cards. The girls were sweet enough to keep her entertained during the days. She napped often, and Jutta walked her around the room several times a day, to get her up and her blood flowing. They'd all been so kind, but she missed David and wished he'd come soon. She looked over at the plate and smiled.

"I think I can eat now. Thank you for taking such good care of me, Jutta." She smiled softly as she took a piece of the sliced tomato and dipped it into the gravy. She groaned in delight. Her eyes rolled up and she closed them, her body rocking happily back and forth.

"Oh, my goodness, this gravy is so darn good."

Jutta tittered, her face turning bright pink with pleasure. "That's my Granny's recipe. My young'uns can't get enough of it."

"Well, you'll have to give me the recipe. I think that when my baby is old enough, I think he'll love it," Mary said, biting into the biscuits and eggs, groaning once more in bliss.

Before she realized it, she'd cleaned her plate. She looked at Jutta in surprise. "I guess I was hungrier than I thought. When will David and the people from the mine be back here?"

"They should be back week after next. They are planning on getting the rest of the folks out of there."

"Oh, that would be wonderful. How are all the children doing?"

"They're good. We found some of their relatives and smuggled some of them back to their homes. Gerhard and I've been talking. Many of the folks coming out of the coal mine, well, they may have to go to families around here until they can get on their feet. We will be donating a lot of our crops to the families who take in those coming out of the mines. Then, next year, they'll be better able to take care of themselves," Jutta said.

"Oh Jutta, that is a wonderful idea. Maybe some of them can help next spring for planting, like a community garden or farm. What do you think?"

"Why, that sounds like a wonderful idea. I'd been lying awake at nights frettin' about the spring planting. We can only get so much planted, and this will help them out as well as ourselves. I'll let Gerhard know. I think that will really work, and help us all out. It'll give hope to those who want to work and feed their families," Jutta said, excited.

She stood, picking up the empty plate.

"I think I'll take a nap; my tummy is so nice and full. Thank you so much for taking good care of me, Jutta."

"It's nothing, and sleep tight, Mary."

Mary was asleep before the door closed.

XXX

Harry, Clay, and Boggy were out in the woods, hunting. Since Boggy had shot the buck, Harry wanted to get out and shoot a few more. They'd separated, though they were each aware of the others' locations. No one wanted to get shot by friendly fire.

Harry and Willene had been discussing bringing in more meat a few days earlier.

"Look," Willene said, "we have a lot of people here. I want to make sure we have a surplus of meat. Besides canning, maybe we can smoke some of the venison, and also make jerky."

"No problem. I'd been thinking of making jerky too. Smoking some is also a great idea. Let's see about what we can do. Earl is out hunting now. Me and the guys will head out in a couple days and see what we can bring down," Harry said.

"Also, keep in mind that, at some point, we can use some of that meat for trading if things settle down eventually."

"Good thinking. I'm hoping that, when we hit Audrey and his people, we'll free the town and ourselves of the threat they pose. Also, we can stop them from taking what little people have."

Harry froze, his mind was drawn back to the present. A buck stood up about thirty feet away. It was a big one and he felt his adrenaline surge. He raised his rifle, let out his breath slowly, and took the shot. It was a good one.

His body relaxed and he walked toward the downed animal. It was a clean shot; the animal was dead. It was a hunter's hope that when he killed an animal, he'd kill it with the first shot. No suffering. No one wanted that. But then, with hunting these men, could the same be said for them? Would he, could he, make them suffer? What kind of man did that make him? He did want them to suffer, but, more than that, he just wanted them gone. He wanted the suffering of others to stop. Perhaps he didn't want them to suffer when he killed them, but Harry was pretty sure that some would want them to suffer, and suffer badly. It was a decision each man had to make, then live with.

He was sure that if someone went after Willene or Marilyn, or Monroe, he'd want them to suffer. But, he thought, unless there was a deep drive to do so, he just couldn't do it. He could kill them sure, with or without them suffering.

XXX

Boney followed Grady, who was roughly a mile ahead and heading out of town. Boney had borrowed Wilber's truck and was keeping well back, his truck lights off. He hoped that wherever Grady was going, he'd get there soon, because it was already early evening. If Boney needed to use the headlights, his plan would have to wait. Boney went slow, stopping every now and then along the side of the road. When he felt safe to move ahead, he drove to catch up, then stopped again, letting Grady get ahead.

Finally, Grady turned off to the left. Boney waited a few minutes before driving slowly toward the turn. It was dusk now and the light was fading fast. He turned left and stopped. There was a house about three hundred feet down a long drive.

Boney backed out. This was perfect. It appeared this was Grady's home. He'd thought he knew the location but had wanted to make sure. There was nothing worse than bad intel. Not to mention going into the wrong house to kill a man. That would not work out well, he was sure. He could come back later tonight and sneak in, explore a bit. He didn't know if Grady had a wife and kids, so it would take some thinking. He wasn't going to hurt women and children, no matter what kind of peckerwood Grady was.

He turned the truck around and headed to Wilber's house. There was some planning to do. No longer needing stealth, he turned the headlights on since it was now full-on dark. It was quiet on the road and he saw no other vehicles. Perhaps he and Wilber should go out hunting tonight, pick off a couple idgits. He was feeling antsy. It had been a while since their last operation. The more they could pick off now, the fewer they had to worry about later. He had some questions for Grady, and he planned to get that intel before he and his people freed the folks down in that coal mine.

He pulled onto Wilber's street and saw the lantern in Wilber's living room window. He smiled. He pulled into the drive and got out. The door to the house opened and he saw Alan's tall, slender figure. He grinned, and Alan stood aside to let him enter.

"What say you, Boney?" Wilber called from his easy chair.

Boney went to the couch and sat heavily, groaning as he did so. Loud pops from his joints echoed in the room as he situated himself. He grinned as Alan brought him a cup of coffee.

"Thank ye, son, and I found out and confirmed where that gomer, Grady, lives. Reckon we'd get him in the middle of the night, take him some place quiet and get a few answers," he said, sipping the hot liquid. It felt good. The nights were becoming cooler and the hot coffee warmed his gut.

"Well now, that's some good news. In the next day or two, or tonight?" Wilber asked.

"I was thinkin' of going huntin' some of his boys tonight, and in a few days to snatch Grady," Boney suggested. "Maybe. What do you think?"

Boney watched as his friend pondered the thought of a hunt that night. Wilber scratched at the stubble on his face. The rasping filled the quiet room, Alan sat quietly, also waiting to hear what Wilber had to say.

"Well, I sure as heck would love nothin' better to take a couple of days to ponder it, but if we're gonna take Grady, we might want to go ahead and do it tonight or, rather, in the early morning. We go pickin' off his men and he'll be on high alert. It'd be harder to get him. Why don't me and you do that tonight?"

"I can drive, and you two get him," Alan volunteered enthusiastically.

Boney looked at the young man and then back to Wilber. He mulled over the possibilities and came to the same conclusion. Wilber was right. Should they knock off a couple booger-eaters, it would just tighten things down more. They desperately needed the intel Grady could provide. Then he and the boys could pick off the others, bring the numbers down. He had names; he just needed locations.

"You're right, Wilber, I know you are. And yeah, we can get that old boy tonight. Alan, you can drive the truck, but you'll stay parked down at the bottom of the drive. Anything goes wrong, you head to your friends and stay there, 'cause they'll come a huntin' for ya," Boney said.

He saw the bright grin on Alan's face. He'd have the boy keep watch, but he'd not let the boy near when they went to interrogate Grady. No child should see that kind of deliberate brutality.

"Oh, I forgot to tell you, I seen Morty Greer, or rather he seen me. I told him that Miss Bella May needed help and wanted protection. I sent him to her. He's a big feller. I hope I did right," Alan said, a worried knot between his brows.

Wilber and Boney both started sniggering, and then out and out laughing. The older men began to cough and sputter. Wilber slapping his knee and rocked back and forth in his lounger, his feet stomping. "That poor bastard don't stand a chance. He ain't the brightest," Wilber said, wiping the tears from his eyes.

"Yeah. That boy's so stupid he fell out of the stupid tree and hit ever' branch on the way down, and then climbed back up and fell back down it again. If I know Bella May, that boy is already planted out back. She used to keep baseball bats scattered about the house after her home got broken into twenty years ago. Then, eight years ago, some poor bastard broke in to her house. He never left. She nearly tore his head off with that bat. That boy's family was all upset and wanted revenge. She told 'em, '*Come on over. I'll cure all your ills.*' Never heard another peep from 'em after that." Boney laughed again.

XXX

Alan sat in the truck, waiting. It was nearly 3 a.m. and his grandfather and Boney had gone into Grady's home twenty minutes earlier. Alan wiped at the sweat beading up on his upper lip. It was nerves; the early morning was damp and cold. He was to wait for the older men to bring Grady to the truck. His grandfather had taken a pillowcase. Alan was not to speak in Grady's presence under any circumstances, and if Grady escaped, Alan was to head to Harry's house and stay put.

Once again, Alan wiped at his upper lip, then he jerked forward when he heard his grandfather's heavy breathing. He detected Boney's too, and muffled grunting. He looked out into the dim night and saw three men heading his way. He got out of the truck and put down the truck's tailgate. Boney had the man by one arm and a long knife pointed at the man's groin. His grandfather had the other arm, and held a long knife to his neck.

Grady's arms were tied behind him, and the pillowcase had been pulled over his head and a rope tied around that. Grady grunted when his hip hit the tailgate. Boney shoved him into the truck bed before climbing up into the back of the truck. He nodded to Wilber, who shut the tailgate. Boney pulled a tarp over Grady's prone body and Wilber jumped into the driver's seat. Alan got back into the truck via the passenger's side.

Wilber pulled away, keeping the lights off until they were well up the road. Alan scooted closer to his grandfather.

"What took so long, Pop Pop?" he whispered into his grandfather's ear. He knew it wasn't necessary, since there was no way Grady would hear them, but he did so anyway. The situation seemed to require it.

"It was a stealthy operation. It took time ta get in ta that house. Then, when we went to the bedroom, he was in bed with his wife. We didn't want ta wake her. Boney put his hand over Grady's mouth the same time I put the knife ta his balls," Wilber said and laughed softly.

Alan looked out of the back window. Boney was leaning against the cab of the truck. He looked back at his grandfather, impressed. "So, his missus never woke up?"

"Naw. She was snorin' away. It was dark, and so we put the pillowcase over his head. He ain't

76

seen who we was. Boney tied him up while I shoved the knife up close and personal to his 'nads. He was real cooperative," he said and sniggered.

Alan scooted over to his side of the seat and looked out the window. He was impressed. His grandpa might be old, but he was cunning and he was good. A soft smile spread across his face as he saw the landscape pass them by. He rolled up the window, now feeling the chill of the night air. He sure was glad he was on the right side of his Pop Pop and Mr. Boney.

There was no sympathy for Grady. In Alan's mind, Grady was responsible for the Lee family's deaths. Katie's mother and father, had been wiped out at his command, not to mention Katie's mother had been raped. He was also sure that Katie would have had the same fate, had Alan not gotten her away from the hospital. Alan also blamed Grady for Robert Santo's death, and his family, leaving Angela orphaned. No, there was nothing but a simmering cauldron boiling within Alan's gut, bubbling with rage.

He'd always been taught to turn the other cheek in church, but he couldn't bring himself to do that. He wasn't sure if he could hurt someone just to hurt them, but he was sure he could kill them if he was defending himself or his Pop Pop, or his friends. No, Alan knew he didn't have it in him to turn the other cheek. He wasn't sure he could kill either, but he'd not let anyone hurt the ones he loved.

CHAPTER FOUR

Monroe ran up and down the front yard, staying well within the roped-off boundary keeping him away from the edges of the woods. No one wanted a repeat of two months ago, when a man had tried to take Marilyn hostage and used Monroe as a shield. He was running up and down, gathering black walnuts and putting them in a basket. The nuts, from the two massive trees were scattered all over the ground, the squirrels having dropped many in their gathering madness.

Earl was with him, sitting on a berm before a fox hole. His long gun lay across his lap as he watched the child run back and forth with such glee it brought a smile to everyone's faces. Harry, Clay, Katie, Willene, and Marilyn were up on the porch, watching the busy antics of the child. Boggy was out on patrol with Brian, Clay's police dog. Charlie was also out with them, though no one figured he'd be anything but company for Boggy.

Angela was on the porch, playing between Willene's feet. These days, she called Willene "Momma." It was bittersweet, for when she'd called Willene that the first time, Willene had wept, a mix of sorrow that Angela would never know her real mother, and joy. Harry sat with Marilyn on the swing, while Clay and Katie had taken the glider.

Harry took note that Clay and Katie were now openly affectionate, holding hands as they talked between themselves. It was good to see. Times were hard, and finding love and being loved was a blessing.

He and Marilyn were also becoming close, but he still had a wall up. It was because of Franziska Gnodtke, his former fiancé, or rather girlfriend, he'd not asked her to marry him yet. She was only former because of his inability to leave this place. It was only been four and a half months ago since he'd said goodbye to Franziska, and yet, it felt as though it had been years. Each day extended, filled with frenetic activity to survive for just one day.

But, after working hard, everything was in place and all could now breathe a sigh of relief. They had plenty of food from the garden; they had three bucks butchered and processed and put away. He'd taken some of the meat to the cave, not wishing to have it all in the house in case they were overrun or attacked by some outside force. Most of their food stores and supplies were still in the cave, with only a week's worth being stored in the old farmhouse.

There had been fewer and fewer run-ins with people finding their way through the mountains. Harry suspected that most were dead, either killed on the road by others or starved to death.

With fall edging out summer, winter would be on its heels. When the temperatures fell, those who'd survived might die if they were not prepared. Life was hard, and every day had to be attended to. One had to think of what needed to be done for today, but also to plan for the future. Winter would be harder for those who'd not done it right. There was very little room for mistakes, and any mistakes could and did kill fast.

He looked over at Marilyn. Her face held a soft smile as she watched Monroe. Getting to know her again after so many years had been eye-opening. He'd only seen her intermittently over the years since high school. But he couldn't bring himself to be more than a friend. For now, life was uncertain. And when they went after Audrey, Yates, and their people, he may not come back. He didn't want to start something, only to die. He also felt guilty and knew he shouldn't, because he thought less and less of Fran these days.

He struggled daily with his emotions, though. Here was a beautiful woman in front of him. Fran would move on with her life, if she hadn't already. Each day, his mind vacillated between the women. He didn't want to act because Marilyn deserved a man who was completely there with his attention and emotions. There should not be the ghost of a woman between them. He would not do that to her.

"I wish I had half the energy of that boy," Marilyn laughed. Harry grinned, his eyes crinkling.

"He makes me tired just watching him," Willene said, rocking slowly in her rocking chair. They were using Marilyn's Wonderbag, a slow cooker without electricity, to make dinner. Harry's stomach rumbled at the thought. A thick venison stew that had been cooking for nine hours. Willene had put a large pan of cornbread in the outdoor oven too. He wished they had fresh milk; he'd love a glass of cornbread and milk. Powdered milk just didn't cut it.

His eyes caught movement up the highway. A truck was headed their way. He recognized it as Wilber's truck, and wondered at the early visit. There weren't many disturbances these days, since it was a very rare vehicle that came past their house. He watched as the truck passed. It carried Alan, in the passenger's side as well as Boney, and Wilber.

Everyone waited for the three to make their way up the hill. Earl joined them, and Boggy stepped out of the woods at the east side of the house, walking up to the porch and joined everyone there.

"Howdy all, how y'all doin'?" Boney called as he lifted his hand in greeting.

Everyone on the porch said "hey," and as the three came up on the porch, Willene went into the house, Marilyn following her. Monroe skipped behind his mother and Katie picked Angela up and placed her between herself and Clay. Boggy and Earl settled on the edge of the porch, each leaning their backs against the thick pillars that supported the overhanging roof of the porch. Alan went to sit beside Boggy and elbowed him. Both young men grinned.

Wilber and Boney shifted the rocking chairs and took their seats as Willene came back out with a large tray of glasses and sweet sun tea. Harry got up and helped her pass around the glasses. Marilyn rejoined them, sitting beside Willene and Harry on the porch swing, and soon everyone was settled.

"Where's Monroe?" Earl asked.

"He's eating his dinner. He'll be out in a bit. I didn't think we'd want him to hear," Marilyn smiled.

"That's probably best," Boney smiled, though there wasn't any humor to be seen in his smile now. He pulled out his pipe and, as though by silent agreement, Wilber, Harry, and Earl pulled out theirs too. Harry saw Willene grin and he winked at her, a smile curving on his lips. Marilyn bumped him and he grinned at her as well. She tittered softly.

The men took a few moments to get their pipes smoldering, and then a comfortable, fragrant fug encircled the occupants of the porch. No one spoke, though the rocking and squeaking of the swing, glider, and rocking chairs made up for the silence.

Monroe came busting through the screen door and grinned like a wild man.

He walked over to Earl, who took out a handkerchief and wiped the stew off the boy's face. The child had stew smeared all over. Monroe kissed the side of Earl's face, then ran off the porch, Charlie hard on his heels. Brian had come up onto the porch earlier and lay curled up at Clay's feet.

"So, me an' Wilber, and Alan too, went on a little recon this mornin'. We snatched up Grady," Boney said and grinned.

Clay barked out a laugh. "He give you much trouble?"

"Not a peep." Wilber grinned. "Naw. Had a knife to his 'nads, pardon, ladies. His wife is a sound sleeper, so we walked him out of his house and took him for a little ride. Some place quiet. You know that old abandoned gas-n-go over on North Fork Road?"

"Sure. It's been closed for years," Clay said, sitting forward on the swing. His arm hung down and he petted Brian on the head. The dog panted, his tongue lolling out of the side of his mouth.

"Now, for I go on, it's gonna get brutal, the tellin'. Anyone here don't wanna hear, might wanna take a powder," Boney said, his voice deadly serious.

Katie got up and kissed Clay on the cheek and smiled. "Sorry, it's just not something I want to know about."

"Me either. I'll go and get things ready for dinner. You boys gonna stay?" Marilyn asked.

Boney and Wilber nodded, smiles peeking around their pipes. Alan's face creased in a brilliant smile, nodding his head enthusiastically.

Marilyn and Katie disappeared inside the house. Everyone kept an eye on Monroe, and Clay picked Angela up, who'd now fallen asleep, and cradled her in his arms. Boggy got up and went to sit beside Clay.

"Well, it weren't pretty. Didn't help that I was still a little mad over Thornton," Boney said.

Wilber snorted. "Yon man knows how ta get some answers, I'll give him that."

Boney grunted and puffed on his pipe. Harry looked over at Alan, who was listening intently. Looked like he hadn't been in the same room when the men had gotten their answers. *That's good. Hearing about it and being there to witness it are two different things*, Harry thought.

"We secured him to a chair and I gave him a couple of head knocks, just to get warmed up. I took the pillowcase off his noggin. He was madder 'n a wet hen," Boney said and chuckled.

"I bet. That man is as vicious as you want. Never did like him," Clay said.

"So, I asked him where his crew held up and where the town's food supply was. That old boy spit on me," Boney grinned. It wasn't a nice grin, Harry noticed.

"So, I took out one of my cigarettes and lit up," Wilber said.

"And I borrowed that roll-up. I gave him a little taste of what he gave my friend. He buckled fast. But of course, I gave him a few more burns, just to make sure he knew I wasn't messin' round. Said most of the boys is held up at Bluemont Bed an' Breakfast. It was Jeff Bluemont's granny's place, but closed down a couple years ago. Looks like the KKK took it over," Boney said.

"We got them sticks. Maybe we could blow 'em up?" Boggy said quietly. Everyone looked over at the young man.

Clay pulled away from him. "Damn, brah, serious, aren't we?" Clay said and sniggered, his hand over his mouth.

Boggy grinned shyly. Harry was glad Boggy was on their side. That was a good idea, blow that place to bits.

"They keep their food stores there?" Harry asked, thinking they'd need to get the food out before they blew it up.

"Naw, Mayor Audrey has it at his house. Greedy gomer. Grady also said they're lookin' for Anderson's stash, said that Andy had the bulk of provisions and had put it someplace, but ain't nobody knows where it is," Wilber said.

"Me and my boys is gonna hit a few of the boys tonight. We know where three are going to be. Bobby White, Darrel Mopes, and Tommy Shipp are gonna be playin' poker at Mopes's house. Gonna pay them a little visit tonight," Boney said and grinned.

"What did you do with Grady?" Clay asked.

"Put him in an empty oil barrel. Anyone opens that, will get a nasty surprise. Grady also said them boys got some gals that ain't wanna be there," Wilber said.

"We aim to send them gals on home to their families. We'll take them boys and anyone else there, down," Boney said.

"Need help?" Harry asked.

"Naw, me an' the boys have been feelin' a little antsy, need to feed that beast." Boney grinned, and Wilber nodded.

Alan looked at his grandfather, scrutinizing him with a speculative gaze. Harry bit his lip, trying not to laugh.

"Grady also said the men are getting disorderly on account they're lookin' for Anderson's stash. Yates seems to be biting at Audrey's ass. A lot of internal squabbling, sounds like. With Anderson having the majority of the haul, Grady thought maybe things might implode. The town is running low on supplies. More like Audrey's been chewin' his way through it," Boney snorted.

"Is there a lot of support for the KKK?" Willene asked, getting up and taking the sleeping child from Clay.

"Grady said there was at first, but then Audrey kept holdin' back on supplies and food. Said sheriff was trying to rein him in. Lot of people died, 'specially the elderly and the very young," Wilber said sadly.

"Now most of the townspeople is afraid of them 'cause they keep coming by, looking for more food. No one has extra to give. Gerhard has been sending food to the town, but I guess only the top boys in the klavern are getting those supplies."

"That works in our favor. I don't think the fine folks from town will get in our way when we go to take them out," Harry speculated. He pulled and puffed on his pipe. He turned when Marilyn and Katie came to the screen door.

"If you want to set out the TV trays for everyone, we can serve y'all some dinner," Marilyn said.

Harry and Boggy got up and went into the house and brought out several TV trays and set them around the porch.

"You don't gotta feed us," Boney announced.

"Speak for yourself, I'm 'bout starved," Wilber laughed. Alan grinned and nodded his head in agreement.

Within a few minutes, everyone was sitting on the porch, quiet for a few moments, enjoying the company. Boggy said grace and everyone dug into the venison stew. Large fluffy squares of cornbread sat on several platters and were passed around, a block of butter on a floral dish as well.

"Where on earth did you get that butter?" Boney asked.

"From the dairy down the road; traded some fresh venison for it," Harry said grinning and winked at Willene. They'd gone down the day after they'd bagged two deer. He and Willene had walked down the road and up the long, winding driveway to the dairy. Joshua Kinkade had met them at a large barbed-wire barricade.

"Trouble?" Harry had asked.

"Little, not so much nowadays. What can I do for you, Harry?" Joshua was a big man, in his early sixties. Harry had known him all his life. He and his mother would get fresh milk, trading eggs for a few bottles, when he was young. Joshua's father had run the dairy back then.

"Got some fresh venison to trade for some butter, if you have any," Harry had grinned.

Joshua had laughed, and they'd both headed to the farmhouse. Joshua explained that they still had about thirty of their dairy cows, but had slaughtered two to eat and preserve for the unforeseen future. It was a small dairy farm, and had become very important.

"I have been thinking, once we get those folks out of the coal mine, we're going to have to relocate some of them. Ones that don't have families. I'll ask Joshua if they can take a family for the winter, perhaps," Harry said.

"Good idea. I'll be askin' around myself, quiet-like. It's going to be a hard winter for all. If we can find that Anderson's food stores, we can ration it out," Boney said.

"I can snoop around. Ain't nobody gonna look twice at me," Alan volunteered.

"Well, just you be careful, grandson. I've grown awful fond of ya," Wilber said and grinned.

"This is some fine stew," Boney said, wiping his mouth with a napkin.

"Would you like more? We have plenty," Marilyn smiled.

"Why yes, ma'am, I would," Boney grinned.

The rest of the late afternoon, everyone sat on the porch, laughing and talking. It had been a long time since they'd had guests and it felt good. It also felt like normal, old times. Once the gas was gone, however, it might be a thing of the past. Harry thought they might want to look into getting a horse. He knew the dairy had a few. It was something to think about. Perhaps they could rig up some kind of small wagon or buggy for the horse to pull.

Twilight was tingeing the sky with lavender and pinks. The mountains blocked out the sun fast, swallowing the light. There was a glow that edged along the rim of the mountains, setting the mountains on fire. Boney, Wilber, and Alan rose to take their leave. Willene came out with two large bags of black walnuts.

"Lord, it's been a long time since I've eaten those. Thanks kindly." Boney grinned. He walked over to Clay and gave him a hug.

"Good hunting, cuz," Clay said and smiled.

Boney giggled like a naughty boy and made his way down the hill. Wilber and Alan stayed behind, talking to Harry.

"We got word to Gerhard about ending the hostage's stay in the coal mine," Wilber said.

"Good. When we do this, I'm hoping we can take the guards out before they get off a single shot. Then I figure we get those folks out and get them tucked away."

"Like I said, we'll make some discrete inquires on places to put them. I reckon most will have a place," Wilber said. He shook Harry's hand, and Alan did the same, grinning shyly. Harry patted the thin youth on the back. He hoped the boy would have luck finding Anderson's stash. That would really help the town through the winter.

He walked back up the hill to the house and watched as Clay disappeared into the woods. He would take the watch after Clay. Coming up on the porch, he heard the women talking in the kitchen, amid sporadic laughter. He could also hear dishes clinking, and figured they were washing up. The light was fading fast, shadows lengthening. The tree frogs began to peep.

He sat in the swing, relaxing into it as he did so. Earl was looking out in the distance.

"What's on your mind, Earl?" Harry asked.

Earl got up from the porch floor and went to sit beside Harry on the swing. "Just wonderin' how many folks is left in town. I wonder how many has died of starvation or from the mayor's people. When we went to see Boney that day, there was nary a soul to be seen."

"I hate to say it, but I suspect the lucky ones were outside of town. Those that lived in town were hit pretty hard, I'm sure, by Audrey's and Yates's people taking what little they had. And if Audrey's been using up those supplies on just his own people, then I'm afraid there may not be many left," Harry said.

"Lord oh mercy, bad enough we lose everything that was modern, but ta also lose because of a greedy peckerwood." Earl shook his head. They both heard the kitchen screen door slam and heard Boggy's deep voice. Harry thought he'd gone to collect eggs from the chicken lot.

"Whoever is left, we'll try to help. Maybe tomorrow, let's see about getting more venison. Maybe we can pass some of that along to help them out when this is over."

"I was wonderin'," Earl said hesitantly.

"What?" Harry encouraged.

"I'm not sure how to ask, but here goes. I'd like to stay on here Harry. I ain't got nothing to go back to. I like livin' here, it feels like my own home," Earl said softly, his voice heavy with emotion.

"Earl, I thought you knew you were welcome," Harry said.

"Well, I reckoned it was just as long as until things quieted down," Earl said. Both men turned as Boggy came out to the porch. He handed each of them a bowl of peach cobbler, then sat in a rocking chair.

"Look, you're all welcome to stay here. This is your home and you're our family now. That means you Boggy, Clay and Katie. Marilyn and Monroe will stay here as well."

"That's good, cause I ain't wanna leave anyhow," Boggy said.

"I'm glad too, I'd miss them young'uns," Earl said, and took a big bite of the cobbler. "And the cookin' too." He laughed.

XXX

It was nearly ten in the evening, and loud, coarse laughter meandered outside Darrel Mopes's house. There were candles all around the living room. Boney and his men, Wilber, Ralph Edison and his twin, Abram, could clearly see through the large bay window. Seven men sat around a table, along with several lanterns gleaming bright and the lights shown through the large window.

Boney, Wilber, Ralph and Abram stood in the yard, looking in. From their vantage point, they saw several young women sat in the several of the men's laps. They didn't look like they wanted to be there. Their body language said they were repulsed.

"Looks like they're drunk," Ralph whispered.

"Yeah. I think we need to go in, weapons hot. Don't see none of their weapons near 'em," Wilber said.

"I'll go in the back door. I already checked an' it's unlocked. I got a good line of sight. Ralph can come with me and Abram can go with you, Wilber. Watch your crossfire. Don't shoot no one unless they go for a weapon. Keep them gals in mind; I don't want any collateral damage. We just want to kill them gomers," Boney said.

Another burst of laughter drew the men's attention. Boney sighed heavily. His heart was pounding, and the adrenaline flowed through his veins. This was different; it was closed in and each man had a hand gun. Their long guns would do no good in close quarters.

"Be aware, fellers, there might be peckerwoods in other rooms. Anyone come out of a room, and it ain't a woman, shoot to kill. Center mass. We'll stay out here a few more minutes. Then we separate, and good luck to you," Boney said quietly.

Each man checked their weapons. Boney could smell the gun oil. He smiled; they were all nervous, but once more felt young, felt needed. He wished Thornton Sherman was there, even though he'd been a Marine. He looked around at the men and nodded. Each had a glint in their eyes, their jaws firm with determination. They separated, and Boney and Ralph crept around back. It was agreed to count to thirty once they got to the doors. They had a better chance of going in at the same time.

His hand on the doorknob, Boney counted down and then pushed the door open. Across the room, he saw that Wilber had done the same. The men at the table hadn't noticed the intrusion yet. They were talking trash and laughing. Boney saw that both Wilber and Abram had their weapons up and aimed at the men at the table. He and Ralph were the same.

One of the young women saw them, and her eyes grew wide. Boney held a finger to his lips and she nodded slightly. She extracted herself from the man's lap and said something about going to the bathroom. When she got up, he smacked her rump. As she walked away, the man noticed Boney for the first time. The man froze, his alcohol-addled mind taking time to process what he was seeing. He stood up suddenly, knocking back the chair and falling over in the process.

The men around the table looked at him and started laughing hysterically. The other woman stood and moved away from the men, suddenly seeing what the downed man had seen. She ran to the back of the house. The men watched her go and then realized they had company.

"Don't move, or we'll open fire," Boney barked in a loud, clear voice that filled the suddenly silent room.

The men around the table did nothing, just stared at the old men surrounding them. All of a sudden, a man with a greasy mullet flew to one side, going for a shotgun. Boney wasn't sure who opened fire first, but the house exploded with gunfire. Cordite stung the nose and smoke filled the air as candles were knocked over. It was over in less than a minute, and all seven men dead on the floor.

"Told ya not to move, you idgets," Boney said, and looked at the other men. They all had startled expressions on their faces, but slow smiles began to spread across their wrinkled faces. They'd done it; they'd killed seven men in less than a minute.

The sound of women crying came to them, and Boney and Wilber went to the back of the house, their guns ready. Wilber opened the door and Boney entered, his gun and eyes scanning the room. Three girls were down in a corner, huddled together.

"You gals okay?" Boney asked.

"Yes sir, are they dead?" a brunette asked.

"Yeah, they're dead. You girls want to go home?" he asked them.

The girls all started crying harder and nodded. They gathered up their things and came out of the bedroom. Boney's nose twitched; it stank in there. The girls preceded him, and he joined them in the living room.

"Ralph, you and Abram look around for food and any supplies that we'll need. Wilber, you go get the truck. You gals sit down. I need ta ask you some questions," Boney said.

The girls held each other and moved as one to the couch. They kept their faces averted from the bodies that lay around the upturned table. Boney sat across from them on the coffee table. The weeping women clung to each other and sniffled and hiccoughed with spent tears.

"Anyone besides these boys know who you are and where you came from?"

"No sir. That boy, Darrel, he got me and my sister, Juney, last week, and got Darla here two days ago. I know our folks is goin' crazy. Worried for us. I'm Alisa," Alisa said, wiping her face on a sleeve.

"So, other than these boys here, no one else saw you?" he pressed.

"No sir."

"Good. Now, we'll take you home. Don't tell no one, except your folks, what happened. We're trying to free this town, but it's gonna take some time. Need to keep things secret. Can you gals keep a secret?" he asked.

The young women all nodded in unison. He smiled at them. They looked thin and tired. If he could kill these bastards again, he would.

Abram and Ralph came into the living room holding several large bags and a pillowcase full of food, toilet paper and other odds and ends. Wilber came back in and began to gather the weapons around the house, along with ammo. He walked over to the couch and nudged Boney. Boney looked up and nodded.

"We'll give you gals the food and guns. Tell your folks to hide it away in case anyone comes snoopin' around," he said kindly. The girls started crying all over again, and the men walked them out to the truck. Boney stayed behind and piled loose debris around the bodies, then poured the alcohol from the bottles over the bodies. Finally, he took one of the candles and lit the papers. The fire spread fast, leaping onto the bodies. He looked around once more, then exited the house. He could hear the crackle of fire follow him out.

The men got into the bed of the truck while the women got into the cab. Wilber pulled out, leaving the flickering house behind.

CHAPTER FIVE

Alan sat in the parked truck for quite a long while. It was quiet and deserted along this stretch of road. His window was down, and he was leaning out of it, his head lying on his propped-up arm. The sun shone down on his face and he closed his eyes, turning it up to meet the meager heat. The days were starting to cool now, and he shivered.

He wasn't particularly fond of winter. But they had a full woodshed out back and their garden had done well. He also had some of the provisions from Mr. Anderson's truck bed. That had been a pure stroke of luck. Being at the right spot at the right moment of his death.

He sat now, in his truck, where he'd seen Mr. Anderson's truck come to its final stop. It wasn't there now, of course; someone had come along to collect it and Mr. Anderson's body. Alan had come to the last place he'd known Mr. Anderson to have been. The man had been heading west. His truck had been full, so Alan reasoned that if he turned and headed east, perhaps he could find where Anderson had stashed the majority of the food stuffs and supplies. If Alan could find that stash before Yates's people, then they could parcel it out to the townspeople and the people from the coal mine once they were freed.

He'd waited for his grandfather to come home last night, unable to sleep. It worried him and made him not a little nervous when his grandfather went out on nightly excursions. He was seeing a whole new side to his grandfather. He'd known the old man had been in the army years ago but had never seen him as anything else other than Pop Pop, an old man. But now, he was seeing the man he used to be, and it was like meeting a new person. That his grandfather had gone out and killed, and in fact enjoyed it, shook Alan up. Boney enjoyed it as well, and both old men took pleasure in it.

He wondered if it was simply the killing of something that needed killing. That made more sense. He knew his Pop Pop to be crotchety at times, but not mean-spirited. And if anyone needed killing, didn't these people? Yes, they'd killed his friend and his family, and left a little girl an orphan. The thought once more caused the anger and rage to roil.

It made him think about, when the time came, if he'd be ready to kill someone. He didn't doubt he could do it. He didn't want to, but he wouldn't shirk from his duty. The KKK had killed many while imprisoning innocent people, putting children and women in the coal mines. Alan was young, but he was no longer naive.

He was pulled out of his woolgathering by blue jays scolding him from an oak tree at the side of the

101

road. He squinted his eyes and looked up into the tree. Sitting here wasn't finding the stash, so he started the truck and made a U-turn. If he went back the way Anderson had been coming, perhaps he'd find a place where the stash might be. There had been quite a bit of food and supplies in the back of his truck that day.

If there was that much, perhaps he should be looking for some place abandoned and large. Someplace people would ignore. He didn't think it would be in a house. Most, if not all, of the abandoned homes had been gone through with a fine-toothed comb. No, Alan reasoned; it had to be some place people wouldn't bother looking.

He drove his truck slow, his head on a swivel. Looking left and right, and slowed when he saw an old barn, the roof stoved-in and the structure leaning. He pulled his truck off the road and parked. Looked around and listened. Turning off the ignition, he got out. He walked up and down the road, listening and looking. He heard nothing but the buzz of insects and birds.

Carefully he walked toward the sad structure, noting the high grass. He didn't see any tread marks from trucks, cars, or humans. He stepped over debris and made his way to the barn. Coming up to the barn, it smelled old, as only old things can. He looked around the perimeter, looking for trampled grass and footprints. He saw nothing. He poked his head into a gap in the gray wooden boards, careful to avoid nails. He'd had his tetanus shot a couple years ago but didn't want to test it. He looked around the dim interior and noticed the brilliant streams of light filtering through the broken roof. Dust motes floated within the golden beam.

The upper story had come down as well. Around the floor, weeds and other grasses grew, but it all seemed undisturbed. He saw abandoned swallows' nests in the rafters, and a sleeping owl. That brought a smile to his face. He had a fascination with barn owls, having seen Harry Potter plenty of times in the past.

Pulling his head out, he stood and looked around. Nothing. He shrugged and turned back to the truck but paused to check his pants for ticks before getting back into the truck. He drove on, still searching and looked around. His mind wandered as he drove. After some time, he passed a dog. It was rail thin. He stopped the truck and got out.

Approaching the dog, he spoke softly. "Hey boy, hey. Where's your momma? You got a dad?"

The dog's tail thumped hesitantly. He read fear and uncertainty in its large, liquid brown eyes. It was a big dog, some kind of mutt. He slowly squatted before the animal, talking nonsense in a soft voice. The dog lowered its large head, but its tail still wagged. Alan put his hand before the dog's nose and let it sniff. The dog did so, then licked

Alan's knuckles. Alan grinned and scratched the dog behind its ears and under its neck. The dog responded by thumping its large tail harder, stirring up the dirt on the ground.

"You wanna come home with me, old boy?" Alan asked. The dog seemed to understand, as the tail wagged faster. Alan grinned broadly now. "What should I call you? You ain't got no collar or tags," he asked the dog and he now stood, the dog's head in both hands as he scrubbed at its ears. It groaned in ecstasy and closed its eyes in bliss at the attention.

Alan laughed and put his forehead to the dog's forehead and blew gently into the dog's nose. He sniggered when the dog licked his face and mouth, and he spat a little when the dog's tongue made it inside his mouth.

He stood looking down at the dog, who looked back up at him. Going to the truck, he pulled out his lunch bag. Willene had given him and his grandfather some of the venison jerky. Pulling out a couple pieces, he turned back to the dog. To his surprise, the dog was right behind him, his head turning, eyes bright. Alan grinned and carefully handed the dog one of the pieces of jerky. The meat was stiff, and the dog had to chew it instead of just gulping it down. That was good, Alan thought. When the dog had finished, he handed it the other piece.

He petted the dog's head, thinking. He'd always wanted a dog but had never had one. This one had the face of a German Shepherd, but not the coloring. He was short haired and had the body and the whipping tail, of a coonhound. Maybe he was a mix? It didn't matter. The dog was his now. He grinned.

He'd have to catch more rabbits and squirrels, but that was okay. It'd be nice to have a friend; life these days was lonesome sometimes. His school friends were either in the coal mine or farther out of town. And even when they were in school, there weren't that many kids. The overall population of Beattyville was about thirteen hundred.

He looked around; he was sure it was less than half of that now. Between starvation and the mayor's people, the population had plummeted. He shook himself out of those dark thoughts. He had to name this boy, and so he named the dog Homer; they'd been studying Homer's Odyssey when all this happened. And hadn't this dog been on an odyssey?

"Okay, Homer, you wanna come with me, boy?" he asked, and patted the seat in the truck. The dog jumped up into the cab with ease. Alan grinned, thrilled that Homer was in the truck. He got in and put his lunch out of reach of Homer. He too wanted to eat. He started the truck and pulled away. After a while he found an abandoned roadside greasy spoon. It was a shack and looked as though it hadn't done well when it was open, whenever that had been.

He got out, but Homer stayed in the truck, watching him. It was a short stop, so when Alan went to the back of the structure, he saw the door had been ripped off. The inside was trashed, and weeds choked the structure; inside leaves and debris were scattered all over the floor. Nothing and no one had been here in months, if not years. He went back to the truck and got in.

After nearly two hours, he pulled over to the side. His stomach was growling. He pulled his bag closer, gave Homer another piece of jerky, and ate some himself. He drank water from his bottle and poured some into his hand. Homer drank from it; he added more, and let the dog drink it. He hadn't thought about how thirsty the dog was.

Pulling back out onto the road, he drove to what looked like overgrown fields. Beyond them stood two rusted out corn or grain silos. The roof of one was hanging down the side, the corrugated metal badly rusted. Alan slowed down and saw two posts with a rusted chain strung between them. He also noticed that one post had been bent over and the ground matted down. He backed his truck up and pulled past the chains, to the far left of the leaning post.

As he drove into the overgrown field, he followed a path; though it was high, he could tell that it had been pushed down recently. It was several weeks since Mr. Anderson had died. His heart began to speed up. Was this where the crafty old man had hidden supplies? He sniggered. If this was it, it was a hell of a good hiding spot. No one would pay this any attention. Why would they? These grain silos looked torn up and rusted out. They held no grain. Anyone passing by wouldn't pay them any heed.

He stopped the truck and got out. He stood, feeling exposed, and looked around, his ears attuned. Nothing. The soft susurrus of the wind blew over the tall grass. Crickets chirped, and he heard birds calling in the distance. It was a lonesome place, quiet. He walked carefully toward the structures, Homer following him, and his hand absently petted the large head. He felt the dog's tongue bathe his hand. He wiped it on his jeans absently. Going around the back, he found a small door, and laughed. It was chained.

"Now why would someone chain an empty silo?" he asked Homer, who cocked his head from side to side. Turning, Alan went back to the truck, pulled the bench seating forward and looked down behind the seat. There was a tire iron, and what he'd hoped for: bolt cutters. He grabbed those and went back to the chain. Slipping the bolt cutter onto the lock, he cut through it. It wasn't hard, a cheap lock.

He pulled the chain from the door and winced; it was noisy. He stopped, looking around. Nothing. He pulled it through the rest of the way more carefully, trying his best to be quiet. Finally, he opened the door, and cringed as it screeched and protested.

His jaw dropped open. Inside, the entire silo was filled with boxes and boxes of food, cans of food, diapers, toilet paper, everything. Tarps covered the stuff, and there were large metal trashcans. He walked over and opened a couple; inside were fifty-pound bags of flour, beans, twenty-five-pound bags of sugar.

His legs felt wobbly. He'd done it! He'd found the stash!

He looked at Homer and felt his eyes sting with tears. This meant life for those in town. Those who really needed it. Not just the KKK. He had to tell his grandfather. They would need to come back with several trucks, heck a whole bunch of trucks. But for now, he figured it was safe enough here.

Only he'd known what Anderson had been carrying the day he died. No one knew he'd had food supplies in the back of his truck, and they certainly didn't know the storage was nearby, just twelve miles from where Anderson had died.

Alan knew that Mr. Anderson had lived on the other side of town, nowhere near this area. No one would be looking here. Alan almost giggled to himself. He left the silo, closing the door behind him, and got back in his truck, Homer beside him. He leaned over and hugged the dog and kissed the large head. Backing out, he left the area quickly. He didn't want anyone knowing he'd been here, otherwise they might snoop around.

His heart raced with excitement and jubilation. It had been a fine day. He had a dog, and he'd found the stash. He leaned over and kissed Homer on his head once more, and scratched under the dog's chin. He got a lick along the side of his face in return.

XXX

Sheriff Yates smashed his fist down on his desk. Officer Tom Learn stood before the desk, his hands in the pockets of his filthy pants. The man was looking at his dusty boots. He was covered in ash and his face was smeared.

"Could you identify the bodies?" Yates asked.

"No sir, they was all charred up. The whole house burned down around them," Tom said.

"You know if it was foul play?" Yates asked, his hands balled into tight fists. First Grady goes missing, now this. He was pretty sure there was foul play, but by whom?

"Can't tell, but we didn't find no weapons. So maybe. The stocks of the guns would have burned, but not the metal, maybe melted a bit, but don't know for sure. Any word from Grady?"

"No. His wife said when she woke up the other morning, he wasn't there. Said there was no sign of struggle, just looked like he got up and left. His truck was still there. Damn it!" He pounded the desk again, causing Tom to jerk.

"Go get cleaned up and gather up the boys. We need to figure out something quick, see who else is missing. Do you know who was at Darrel's house? Seven bodies you said, right?"

"Yes sir, seven, and don't know who else was at the house. There was melted poker chips on the floor, think he had a game going. Oh, and ain't no one seen Morty, lately."

"Well shit. All right, see about gathering up the men. Let's see if we can't figure this out," Yates said, now tired.

"Should I tell the president?" Tom asked.

"Hell no, and don't call him president, 'cause he ain't. Just go gather the men. We need to figure this out fast, before we lose more people."

Yates watched as Tom left the office. He let out a long sigh. The boys had been playing poker, which meant drinking. Could it have been an accident? Tom had said they were all laid around in a group; if the fire had started, they would have left the house or put it out. No, someone had surprised them and killed them. With seven men, they must have been out numbered. Could the townspeople be turning on them? He'd not be surprised if they were. People were getting desperate. Their own supplies were getting low.

He'd had some of his men go out and hunt. But they couldn't live off meat alone. Thankfully they had Gerhard's produce coming in. They were due another delivery at the end of the week. That was good. Plus, they still hadn't found Anderson's stash. That cagey bastard had hidden it well. There was no telling where he'd put it. They'd torn his house and all the outlying buildings on his property apart. Nothing. It had all turned into a shit show.

They hadn't worked together with the townspeople, and by doing so had alienated them. Some goddamn great plan. He needed to talk to Audrey; they needed to come up with a better strategy, or none of them would survive the long winter. He got up and left his office. Outside the building, he took a look around.

The streets were eerie and deserted, there were fewer people to be seen. Trash danced along the street, which had been spotless before this mess had happened. First Vern, now Grady and Morty. Did they just bug out? There had been no clues, no bodies.

It was a short walk to the courthouse. His frustration mounted when he saw men just sitting around.

"Get your ass out there and look for that stash of Anderson's. You're doing me no good here," he said to a short, slender man with dirty blond hair who'd been picking his teeth with a bent-out paperclip.

The sullen man looked up. Heat filled Yates when he continued to sit there.

"President gives the orders," he said with a sneer.

"Get your sorry ass out there now, before I put a bullet between your useless fucking eyes," Yates roared, and kicked the man's feet hard, causing the smaller man to nearly fall out of his chair. The other men jumped out of their chairs and left the courthouse. The smaller man got up, shooting Yates a look that told Yates he'd need to watch his back.

Audrey came out of his office, face florid, food bulging out from his cheeks. Yates watched as Audrey's beady eyes took in the scene.

"What in tarnation is goin' on here?" Audrey said, crumbs flying out of his mouth.

"These people are useless, Rupert! They need to get off their asses and start looking for Anderson's stash. We are getting seriously short on supplies. We aren't going to make it through the winter if we don't find them," Yates barked, still looking at the thin man, who'd yet to leave.

"Well damn it, these are *my* men," Audrey said indignantly.

"I tried to tell him, Mr. President," the thin man sneered, giving Sheriff Yates an eat shit look.

"You're just the sheriff; you need to leave my people alone and get your own people after this problem," Audrey ordered, a fat hand coming up to wipe away the crumbs.

Yates stood silent for a moment, looking from Audrey to the smaller thin man, who had a satisfied smirk on his face. Yates took in a deep breath, closed his eyes. He heard the man behind him snickering. Yates opened his eyes, turned around, drew his service revolver and shot the man between his eyes. He was so close to the man, he felt the warm spray of blood as the man flew back and onto the floor. Yates turned around and shot Audrey between the eyes as well.

He turned, wiping at his face as two men came running back into the courthouse. He held the gun at them, and they immediately came to a halt. His blue eyes seemed to burn; he could feel them almost pulsing as he looked at the three men before him.

"Who do you work for?" he asked them.

They looked at the bodies, then the gun pointed at them, then into Yates's eyes.

"We work for you, sheriff," they said in unison.

"Good, now get these bodies out of here. Go through this place and get every scrap of food that little bastard has been hording and take it to my office. I want you three to go through this building and look for anything useful. Any weapons, anything, and bring to my office. Do it now," he ordered, when the men stood immobile for a long moment. They jumped to his command and went past him.

Sheriff Yates left the courthouse and walked back to his office. It was though a weight had been lifted off his shoulders. He saw Tom, Reece Archer, and Jeff Bluemont running toward him. He held a hand up, signaling all was well.

"We heard shots," Tom puffed, his face pale.

"I just cleaned house. Audrey is out, that useless tub of lard," Yates said mildly.

Tom looked at him, as did the other men. Then he nodded. They followed Yates to his office. All the men took a seat.

"Here is the situation. Vern, Morty, and Grady have gone missing. I don't know if it was foul play or if they just got the hell out of Dodge. There aren't any bodies. What I do know is that someone has picked off quite a few of our people. Darrel Mopes and six others were killed. Not sure who was with him. I need you men to check around. Someone has seen something. Also, get people out

114

there looking for Anderson's stash. He had most of our supplies."

"I'll get Ralph and Murphy, and we'll see what we can do, sheriff," Officer Tom Learn said. He and the other men left.

Danny Yates looked out his window, watching the men as they moved away quickly, talking rapidly. He shook his head. Small niggles of fear began to lick at him, like a small weak flame. He knew it wouldn't take much to get a roaring fire going. He was losing control, if he'd ever had it in the first place. Could they have done something different? He just didn't know.

XXX

Clay and Katie walked around the large property holding hands, enjoying the quiet and solitude. It was Clay's turn for patrol but, as had become their custom, they went together. Neither minded the double duty; they were together, and that was all that counted. The dogs were off sniffing in the woods. It was peaceful.

"What do you think we should do when all this is over?" Clay asked Katie, who had squatted down, looking at mushrooms.

She looked up and smiled at him, and he could see love in her dark eyes. He couldn't help but smile back. She had a leaf caught in her hair, her cheeks were pink, and she looked like a wild nymph in the woods.

"I was thinking that we should move back to town," she said.

"Really?" Clay was surprised.

"Once this is all done, the town is going to need a doctor. I'm not sure if anyone is left from the hospital. The people will also need a sheriff, not some corrupt madman. I think they'll need you, Clay. You're one of the most honest men I know."

"Thanks, honey, but I think, as honest as I am, I am a little one-sided when it comes to you. And you just might be blinded by my good looks and sparkling personality," he said. "I guess you're right, however. I hate to leave here, though. It has been a home and has felt like home." He pulled her up and removed the leaf from her hair. His eyes crinkled when she stood on her tiptoes for a kiss.

"It has felt like home, and I do hate to leave. But they won't need us here. The town will. We can find a nice home in town. I hate to say it, but I'm sure there are a lot of abandoned homes there. We can find one and make it our own. With the supplies found, we can at least survive the winter until we can plant in spring," she said.

They walked for a while, each in their own thoughts. They watched as the dogs played and chased each other through the undergrowth. The distant rhythmic drumming of a woodpecker echoed off the mountain. The songs of the chickadees and several warblers reached them, their melodic refrains pleasing. Clay took a deep breath. He was sure he'd miss this place, but Katie was right. They needed to help the townspeople recover from the brutality that was forced upon them.

Perhaps they could find a house with a little land and some woods. That would be nice. Some place Brian could run and move freely. He didn't think the dog would like to go back to apartment living. He seemed to thrive outdoors.

"Okay. When all this is done, we'll find us a place, and you can set up shop at the hospital and hang out your shingle." Clay grinned down at her, pulling her in. He felt her slender arms wrap around his waist and hugged her hard.

"Okay, and you can set up and guard and protect us. And run the law as it should be," Katie said, and kissed him.

XXX

Alan turned onto Walnut Street and saw a blockade ahead. It hadn't been there earlier that morning, and his hand gripped the steering wheel. There were only two men, but thcy had guns and were eyeing his truck and talking excitedly between themselves. Alan looked over to his new pet.

"I think we need to get. Them fellers look like they want Pop Pop's truck," he told Homer, who licked his face. Alan grinned and looked back at the two men; they were walking toward him.

"Get out of that truck, son," a tall thin man yelled from roughly thirty feet away.

"I can't. It's my Pop Pop's truck," he yelled back.

A short fat man laughed. "Not any more, it ain't."

"That's what I reckoned," Alan said, and put the truck in reverse and spun around impressively. Homer flew to the truck floor and Alan yelled out an apology to him. He stepped on the gas and flew away from Walnut Street. Glass shattered behind his head. He could hear gunshots, and he leaned heavily over, trying to duck out of the way. Homer was trying to scrabble back up onto the seat.

"Stay down, Homer, or you'll get shot by them assholes," Alan shouted, trying to push the dog down with one hand. There were more shots, and the metallic ping from hits to the truck's body. It didn't take long before he was out of the area, turning down one street and then another. His heart slammed painfully in his thin chest. He patted the seat, encouraging Homer to climb back up.

He looked in the rearview mirror and saw no sign of pursuit. He grinned at the dog and reached a hand over to pet the large head. The dog's whip-like tail thumped on the seat. "We sure did git lucky, huh, boy?" he asked.

Then he coughed and pain shot through his side. He looked down and was surprised to see blood on his left side. He slowed the truck and pulled to the side of the road. He shifted, saw the pool of blood on the seat, and lifted his shirt and coat. Blood slowly leaked from his body. He suddenly felt nauseous at the sight.

"I need ta get ta Harry's, so Dr. Katie can patch me up," he told Homer, looking at the gas gauge. Quarter tank; he sure hoped it was enough to get him there. He pulled back on the road, increasing speed. Damn them boys anyway. He looked over at the dog, wondering if he'd die and not have a pet after all. He then thought, with sorrow, that his Pop Pop would be all alone without him.

That made him go faster. He was getting closer. He checked the gauge again. It was down, and he wasn't sure if he was going to make it. He'd wasted a lot of gas going slow while looking for Anderson's stash. He had to make sure someone knew where the supplies were. He couldn't let all that food go to waste. Too many people needed it.

He had to slow down on the switchback curves. The things had never bothered him before, but now they ate up precious gas. Dark spots were now starting to sprinkle his peripheral vision. He knew that wasn't good, cause he'd seen on TV that people fainted from that. Or did they die? He wasn't sure. At least it didn't hurt too much, just when he twisted on the curves. His eyes darted once more to the gas gauge. Lower still. *Dang it*, he thought.

At least he was only a couple miles away. He held his breath as he took the last curve. It was a sharp one and he had to slow down. It hurt his side and he gritted his teeth. The truck straightened out and he could see the house up ahead. The truck began to complain, then knock and bang. Then it stopped.

"Guess we gotta walk the rest. Come on, Homer, you're gonna meet some good friends of mine," he said, and slid out of the truck, his knees buckling. He caught himself on the door and pulled himself up. The seat was pooled with blood, his blood. He felt a thrill of fear rush through him. The dark spots were taking up more space around him, like scary ghouls. He took a step, then two, his legs firming up beneath him. He took hold of Homer's scruff, afraid to let go.

He took another step and then another. He could see people on the porch, but for some reason he couldn't make out who they were. The spots were getting darker, but Alan forced himself to take another step, then another. He thought he was doing pretty good; his legs were moving, but he wasn't exactly sure why his cheek was on the pavement. Homer was whining and licking his face, but he could feel his legs still walking. Then the dark spots ganged up on him and he was gone.

XXX

Alan blinked his eyes open. Things were kind of dark around him, and he wondered if he'd overslept. Then Dr. Katie's face came into focus and he grinned up at her, his face heating up. *She sure is pretty*, he thought. She smiled back down at him, and he felt his heart flutter with joy.

"Hey, Dr. Katie," he said. His words came out slurred. He frowned.

"Hi, Alan, are you okay?" she asked him softly.

"I am now." He blushed profusely, then noticed other faces looking down at him.

"What? What happened?" he asked, confused.

"Looks like you were shot. You damn near bled to death," Harry said, his voice deep and filled with worry, which was reflected in his face.

Alan looked and saw a bag hanging from a lamp, and followed it down to a needle in his arm. Nausea gripped at him, making him giddy. He'd always hated needles, and now he was hooked up to an IV. He tried to sit up, but Dr. Katie held him down. Her hands were warm on his chest, though he felt quite cold.

"Stay down, Alan. You lost a lot of blood. The bullet didn't hit anything major, but it did nick a large vein," she said.

"What happened, Alan?" Harry asked, and Alan saw Clay behind him.

"I found Anderson's stash!" he said excitedly, and tried to sit up once more. Again, hands pushed him back.

"Really? Where? And who shot you?" Clay asked.

"I found two old rusted grain silos over on Cherry Branch Road, about twelve miles up on the left. The silos are in an overgrown field, but there ain't no houses around," Alan said.

He suddenly felt nauseated. It must have shown, as Dr. Katie brought a bowl up to his face and he immediately vomited. He felt his face heat with shame. He kept his eyes closed as she wiped his face clean. Then he felt a cold glass of water pressed to his lips.

"You okay, son?" Harry asked.

"Yeah. Where's Homer?" Alan asked suddenly, looking around frantically.

"That your dog? He's outside. We fed him. He looked a little skinny. He didn't want to let us take you," Harry said, a smile in his voice.

"I found him. He's my dog now. I was headin' home and got stopped on Walnut Street. They done put up a blockade. They wanted my truck, so I ran away. But guess they done shot me and the truck. I ran out of gas." He paused a moment. "I need to get home." He once more tried to sit up. Hands pushed him back down.

"We'll go let your grandfather know, and we'll fill up the truck and return it," Harry said.

"You're not going anywhere for a while, so you might as well get comfortable, young man," Katie said, tempering the order with a smile.

Alan grinned back at her and nodded meekly. He suddenly felt tired, so closed his eyes.

CHAPTER SIX

Harry and Clay drove past the dead truck. They'd get gas and bring it back to put into Wilber's truck. The important thing was to let Wilber know Alan was safe. They were also going to take care of the men who'd shot a teenage boy. Harry's rage was tamped down, and he looked over at Clay's stony countenance.

It was dusk. By the time they got to town, it would be full on dark. They didn't have to worry about anyone seeing Clay; he had a ball cap on and his jacket was pulled up to nearly obliterate his face. And if they did see him and they were the wrong people, Harry would make sure they'd tell no one.

He was in a dark mood and wanted to take it out on one of those assholes. He hoped that whoever had shot the kid was still there. He marveled at Alan's strength. The kid had been more concerned about getting word to them about the supplies than his own life. Alan was young but had the makings of a great man. Harry hoped the boy lived long enough to fulfill that promise.

He took the curves slowly, expecting barricades. The streets were empty when they made it to town and they drove quietly, neither man speaking, lost in their own thoughts. Harry pulled out his Glock, taking note that Clay had pulled his service revolver; they were getting close to Walnut Street. This was the normal route to Alan's home, though there were other ways. Ahead, two cars had been pushed together to block the road. There was a metal trashcan with a fire burning inside. A grim smile flitted over Harry's face when he saw two men step out. A tall thin man, as Alan had described, and a shorter, stockier man.

Harry rolled down his window, as did Clay. He slowed his vehicle and stopped fifteen feet away. He leaned his head out.

"What's going on here?" he called.

"You need to hand over that truck, mister." The tall thin man grinned. His long gun was cradled in his arm lazily, but not pointed directly at Harry.

Big mistake, thought Harry.

"Really? That's just crazy. By who's authority?" he asked conversationally.

The tall man sniggered and looked at his partner. Then he looked back at Harry.

"By my authority. Now get out," he said, and began to raise his weapon. Harry and Clay brought their weapons up simultaneously and leaned out their windows. Harry's was the first to discharge, and the thin man's body crumpled with two shots to the chest, blood blooming black in the night. Clay double-tapped the stockier man, one in the chest and one in the neck. Blood oozed out and neither

man moved. Harry and Clay got out of the truck and
walked over to the downed men.

Both were still alive, their labored breathing
causing bubbles to foam from their mouths and
noses, the silence of the night broken by their
gurgling sputters. Their eyes widened when they
saw Clay. Harry saw that Clay was grinning, as he
squatted down.

"Ni... ni..." the thin man tried to say, then
died. The shorter man's lips moved, but no sound
came out. The wound in his neck spurted in thin jets
across the road. Clay had nicked the artery.

Clay stood and looked at Harry. Harry saw the
grim, satisfied smile on the taller man's face. He
was sure that his own visage reflected the same
satisfied look, because he was damned happy.
They'd got the shit-heels that had shot a teenager.

"Two less assholes in this world. Let's go find
Wilber," Clay said. He picked up the weapons
dropped by the dead men, then patted both men
down. It didn't take him long to remove the
ammunition stuffed in their pockets.

Harry nodded, and both men walked back to
the truck. Harry did a U-turn and took another route
to Wilber's home. In five minutes or so, they turned
into the driveway. Both men looked over to the
burned-out remains of Katie's home next door. It
was dark, but the headlights illuminated the plot,
and the burned-out shell of the house. What had

once been a neat, well-kept home was now a gruesome caricature of a dwelling. It summed up the whole disaster that had befallen their town. Wanton and depraved destruction, a singular disregard for humanity.

"I don't want Katie to see this. She shouldn't have to see this ugliness," Clay said softly.

"I agree. You know you and Katie are welcome to stay at the farmhouse once we clear all this up. Also, once we lose gas, we will pretty much be stuck out there. I'm looking ahead, thinking about getting a horse, trading some of our supplies, maybe for a buggy or wagon, so we can travel to town," Harry said as they walked up to Wilber's house.

"Katie and I've talked. I think we will move into town. I want to take over as sheriff, and the town will need a doctor. I'm hoping we can find an abandoned home with a big enough plot of land to plant for the spring," Clay said.

Harry nodded, lifting his hand to knock on the door, which opened before he could. Wilber looked at each of the men, a shotgun held at ready.

"What in tarnation are you doin' here? Where's Alan?" he asked, worried.

"He's safe, Wilber. He's up at the house. He was shot. We killed the men who did it on our way here. They'd set up a barricade over on Walnut Street," Harry said as he entered the gloom of the house. Several lit hurricane lanterns stood on the kitchen table. He and Clay walked over, and all three men sat down.

"They shot my grandson? Why?" Wilber asked, torn between rage and grief.

"They wanted his truck. Alan said he did a U-turn and hauled ass. He said the men shot at him. He got to my place just as his gas ran out. We saw him get out of the truck and then he fell. Clay and I picked him up in our truck and the women took care of him. He's now basking in their care," Harry said, trying to ease Wilber's worry.

"Can we go? Can I see my grandson?" Wilber asked, getting up from the table and looking around franticly.

"Sure can. We'll need to fill up a couple of gas cans on the way so we can get your truck running again," Harry said.

Wilber got his jacket and went to Alan's room. When he came back, he had a change of clothing for the boy. He blew out the lanterns and all three men left the house. It was full dark and no moonlight, the clouds heavy with the promise of rain.

Wilber went to his shed and opened the door. He pulled out a two-gallon and a five-gallon gas can. He handed them to Harry, who put them in the back of his truck. Wilber climbed into the truck and Clay got in beside him.

"Alan found Anderson's stash, by the way," Clay told Wilber, a smile spread across his face.

"He did? Oh, my grandson is a sharp one," Wilber laughed. Harry heard the immense pride in the old man's voice.

"You also have a new dog," Harry sniggered, looking over at the old man.

"What? What dog?" Wilber asked.

"It seems that Alan found himself a dog, a big one, and it loves the boy," Clay laughed.

"That's okay. My grandson has earned it." The old man shook his head. "I can't believe he found the stash. That's gonna help a lot of folks around here."

XXX

Katie brought a bowl of broth out for Alan; she didn't want him on solid foods until they had been able to check his stool. She wanted to make sure there was no blood, indicating a nick in the bowels. They'd have to watch him closely, but as far as they'd been able to ascertain, the bullet hadn't hit anything vital.

The bullet had been slowed considerably by passing through the layers of steel in the truck, and the seat upholstery. They would have to watch out for infection, though she and Willene had irrigated and cleansed the wound as thoroughly as they could. She dug the slug from his body and thankfully it hadn't gone deep. She still had antibiotics available and would give him a run. With that, he should recover fully.

She looked down at the boy, who was sleeping. It was important to get him eating and moving his bowels. She placed a gentle hand on his forehead, causing his eyes to open. He wasn't hot, and for that she was glad.

"Hey, Dr. Katie," he said softly, smiling up at her.

"Hey, Alan. How are you feeling, honey?" she asked.

"I hurt, but okay."

"I have some broth. You think you could eat?"

"Yes'm, I think I could."

She helped him sit up, and he grimaced with pain. She apologized, but he grinned and waved it off. She plumped the feather pillows behind him, then began to spoon in the broth. Homer was by the couch now and watched as Katie fed the teen. She looked down at the dog and his tail thumped on the floor

"I can feed myself, Dr. Katie," Alan protested.

"I know, but I want to. Do you mind?"

He grinned widely. "No ma'am."

"I think Homer is worried about you. He seems like a good dog," Katie said.

"Oh, he's a good dog, an' smart too. I like him a lot. I ain't never had a dog. He's just perfect," he said and sighed happily, causing Katie to grin.

When she'd finished, she took note that the boy looked tired and worn out. She helped him lie back down, and left him, heading back into the kitchen. Earl sat at the kitchen table with Monroe in his lap. Both were eating dinner, fried chicken, fried potatoes, green beans, tomatoes, and a vinegar coleslaw. Monroe had a small portion of macaroni and cheese, his favorite.

Willene was holding Angela in her arms. Katie could have sworn the child had more food on her face than inside. Willene also had food covering her. She put the child's fingers into her mouth and cleaned them, and Angela giggled. Katie smiled. She was going to miss this, but once things were safe, the town would need her.

Willene and Marilyn were more than capable of taking care of everyone here. She'd miss them, but she and Clay had already decided they wanted to begin their lives in town. They wanted their own home to raise their children. They had each other and that was enough.

"They'll need a sheriff. I'm hoping Stroh will be there as well. We can build a new police force. It doesn't have to be large, but it has to be honest and humane," Clay had said on their walk back up to the house.

131

She hoped this would end soon, that the KKK would be taken out, never to rise in their small town again. The world no longer had room for that kind of hate. They all needed each other to work together, to build something better than before. She'd have to go back to the hospital, and hopefully there would be enough supplies and medicines there that she could help folks.

She also thought that, when she got back to town, she'd head to the local library. She really hoped no one had destroyed it. She'd find books on natural cures and herbal medicines. At some point, the medicines at the hospital would run out, and she'd have to learn new ways of treating people. It would give her something to do over the long winter. She enjoyed learning about new methods of healing.

Boggy walked in, pulling her out of her thoughts. As he walked by Earl and Monroe, he squeezed the child's head playfully, eliciting a giggle from the boy. Marilyn grinned, and took the NVGs from Boggy, and took his gun as well. She walked over to Earl and patted him on the shoulder, then leaned over and kissed Monroe on his head.

"I'll be back in a while. You listen to Uncle Earl and Aunt Willene, okay?" she warned her son.

"Yes ma'am," he said and smiled up at her.

Boggy took Marilyn's seat, and Katie went over to dish him up a plate of food, and one for herself.

"How's Alan doin'?" Boggy asked Katie.

"He's good. He ate some broth and now he's asleep. No temperature, and I checked the stitches. There's just a little redness, nothing serious. His dog is beside him, on the floor," she said.

"I can't believe that boy found Anderson's stash," Earl said, shaking his head.

"Me either," Boggy echoed.

"I'm not surprised, really. He's a smart boy," Katie said, handing Boggy a plate and sitting down beside him.

"He is that, and brave as well," Willene said as she took a cloth napkin and began to clean Angela up.

"Yes, he is, and he doesn't give up either," Katie said. There was a round of soft chuckling in the kitchen. It was warm in the room, from the fire in the stove and the companionship of the people.

"That stash will surely help the remaining townspeople, and those that come out of the coal mine. Does anyone know how many are down there?" Willene asked no one in particular.

"Wilber said they're thirty of 'em left, without the young'uns," Earl volunteered.

"I wonder how they're going to be housed for the winter? And fed, though with the supplies

133

found, I think that will go a long way in helping," Katie said.

"I believe there are many who have relatives. And I think, with the promise of supplies, some will be willing to open their homes. I think some will go back to their own homes, if they've not been burned down," Willene said.

"Clay and I've been talking. Once we get this mess settled out, we plan to go back to town, find us a vacant home and live there. They'll need a doctor and police force there. And, though I'll miss you all, I think the town will be needing us," Katie said, reading surprise and sorrow on the faces around her.

"I sure wish you'd both stay here, but I understand," Willene said.

"I don't know if Harry said anything, but me an' Boggy is gonna stay on here, if that's alright?" Earl commented, worry written all over his face. Katie saw Willene grin, and she smiled as well.

Willene reached over and hugged Earl. "You and Boggy are welcome. You're our family, as are Katie and Clay, no matter where they go," she said with a smile.

Shadows flickered over the group's faces. The hurricane lanterns brightened up the kitchen, but also left it in heavy shadows. They all turned when they saw headlights coming up the hill. Harry was back. Katie picked up her lantern and went out to the living room. She was sure Wilber had questions.

XXX

Everyone sat out on the porch later that evening. The kids were asleep upstairs, and Wilber had been fed dinner and invited to spend the night. Harry could see the glow of pipes along the porch and the glow of a cigarette, Earl. The tree frogs were singing, but a little subdued. There was a light rain coming down and it was chilly. Everyone had a jacket on, and a blanket thrown over their laps.

It was quite cozy in the dark and quiet. Harry would go out in a few hours to walk the property. He now had the NVGs in his lap and peered through them from time to time. He wasn't very worried; there were fewer incidents these days.

"It sure is peaceful up here," Wilber said softly, unwilling to disturb the hushed atmosphere.

"It is. Our family picked a good place to build a house. We can see a good ways up and down the road, and we're high enough that the traffic never reached a high pitch here. Now, it never will," Willene said just as softly.

"I was thinking about talking to Joshua about getting milk and butter for the townspeople. First, I'll have to trade for a horse and see about a wagon or buggy. I think our gas will only last another month or so before it becomes either too degraded to work or is completely gone. If I had a diesel, I would have been able to make the vehicle last longer," Harry said.

"I could ask Boney. He knows a few folks with some horses. Maybe make a good trade. I also think Boney has an old buggy, or wagon. It ain't much, and might need repairs, but we'll see what we can do. That old bus they're using ta get them folks back and forth from the coal mine to Gerhard's farm is diesel. We could maybe use that to get folks around. I'm sure there must be a mechanic somewhere in town," Wilber said.

"That's a great idea. Maybe come this way every few weeks. Or we can go to town for a visit and trading," Willene said.

"That would be wonderful. I'd miss you guys so much if you didn't come," Katie said.

"Once this mess with the mayor and Yates is done," Harry said.

"Mayor's dead. Heard tell, Yates done shot him 'tween the eyes." Wilber laughed low.

"Well, that is one less idgit we gotta worry about," Earl said and laughed.

"I wonder what brought that on?" Marilyn asked.

"Probably tired of listening to that idiot. Yates doesn't suffer fools easily, and if you've spent any time near the man, you'll know he's a pontificating fool," Clay said in disgust.

136

Harry laughed, and soon everyone else joined in. Harry felt Marilyn shiver and scooted closer, adding his blanket to hers so they overlapped. He heard her soft thanks. They were on the swing. It felt normal and natural for them to be there together. It had become, of sorts, a habit.

The group quieted down once more, each lost in their thoughts. They heard Alan cough, and Katie and Wilber got up and went into the house. Harry heard them murmuring quietly. Their voices didn't sound stressed, so his shoulders relaxed.

He brought the NVGs up to his eyes and scanned around. They managed okay with light rain but were useless in a downpour. He heard the dogs, their snoring had picked up, and chuckled softly. Homer was inside with Alan and wouldn't leave his side. Wilber had petted the dog upon meeting him.

"Are we going on Friday?" Clay asked quietly.

"Yeah. We'll leave out of here around four. The bus usually gets back to the coal mine around six. We can park a little ways out and walk in. It might be tricky, as there isn't a whole lot of cover, but I'm bringing my rifle. I was thinking about hitting them just as the bus was arriving. That way, their attention is diverted," Harry said.

"Sounds good. If there are only two guards, shouldn't be that difficult to take them out. If things are good, you might take them out before the bus arrives," Clay said.

"Then what?" Earl asked.

"We get those people out of there and take them either back to the farm or divide them up and get them to their families. I figure the bus can take them to wherever they need to go. Once that's done, we'll head to the Bluemont Bed and Breakfast and see about blowing that up. I'd rather not, only because of the surrounding homes. If there aren't too many there, we can take them out with our weapons," Harry said.

"I can talk ta Boney, see 'bout putting someone reliable to watch the place and keep track of their coming and going," Wilber said, coming out of the house.

"That would really help. Do you think you and Boney can take out a couple more of Yates's people?" Harry asked.

"Sure can. It'd be our pleasure. Got a couple of them peckerwoods in mind, pardon ladies," Wilber said and Harry grinned in the dark. He heard Marilyn's soft snigger. He elbowed her softly and she nudged him back, now giggling softly.

Katie came back out and sat beside Clay, who lifted his quilt. She slid under it.

"Alan okay?" Willene asked.

"Yes. I checked his wound, and it's doing good. No temp yet, so that is good as well."

"How soon can he come home?" Wilber asked.

"I want him here for at least another three days. I want to make sure there are no surprises. By then, he should be able to get up and move around," Katie answered, her voice kind.

Gunfire resounded in the distance. It was rare these days. Harry figured someone was hunting, he hoped an animal, not human.

"Wonder if they're huntin' deer?" Boggy echoed his thoughts.

"Might be. Maybe a deer made the mistake of going into their garden," Clay said.

"Just hope it wasn't someone hurtin' someone else," Earl said quietly. There were grunts of acknowledgment around.

"Violence is slowing down in the mountains, I think. Most are dead or have taken care of those who were violent. There aren't any more people, that I can tell, coming from Lexington. Unless they can find a vehicle and enough gas," Harry said. He pulled on his pipe; the damp air was causing the pipe to die.

"Yeah. Hopefully we won't have to worry about anyone coming from that way. I really do hate to think what it has been like in that city, or any other cities, for that matter," Willene said.

"I don't even want to imagine what it was like in Chicago, or New York. I'm sure there must be disease, like typhoid, cholera, dysentery, and God knows what else," Marilyn said.

139

"No, I'm sure life in the big cities killed thousands, if not millions," Katie said.

"We've had our own struggles here, and heartbreak and tragedies, but I think elsewhere it has been on a massive scale and, because it is so big, I think that it more than likely spread, like a cancer, to the smaller towns near the edges of those big cities," Harry said thoughtfully.

"There is something to be said about living remotely," Clay said, and grunts of agreement sounded around the group.

XXX

Vern felt a shiver go through his body. He'd lost track of time, but it seemed the cold was seeping into the basement more and more. It was dark, and he could smell himself and Morty. He was keenly aware of the vicissitude of his situation. He had no more control of it than he did his bowels. Morty was quiet for now, thank God. The man didn't know when to shut up.

He didn't know if it was today or yesterday, but Morty had gone apeshit. Vern figured the man had finally come to the conclusion he was going nowhere fast. He'd started screaming and cursing, the sound of it hurting Vern's ears. He'd tried to tell the idiot to quiet down, that it would only piss Bella May off. That didn't help. When the door above opened up and the bright light of the solar lantern shown down, Morty renewed his hysterical rant. Vern had been impressed with his companion's vocabulary.

Bella May came down the steps, lantern and a pair of poultry shears in hand. Vern had felt a wave of cold filter through his body, as it almost invariably meant no good was about to happen. He'd tried to warn Morty, but the man was pure up stupid. Hobo hadn't been bright, but he knew when to keep his mouth shut. He watched, his body shivering with both cold and dread. Bella May walked over to Vern, and he tried to shrink back.

"Did you tell him to shut up, Vern?" she asked, her voice mild. But he could see the glitter of anger in their green depths.

"Yeah, I tried. I don't think he is as bright as Hobo was," he'd said.

Bella May snorted at that and turned to go over to the still-ranting Morty. She stood in front of the man while he continued to scream and spit expletives at the old woman. Even now, Vern shook his head at the memory. Bella May had stood there, listening to the man. Morty's face was red and both his hands missing. Bella May had cut them both off the first day.

"So you don't get the idea of breaking free, next I'll be taking your feet. You're a big boy, and I can't take the chance of you getting out of here," she'd said. Then she'd smiled and proceeded to cut

141

the man's hands off. Morty hadn't passed out, and had screamed the whole time. Vern's head had pounded for hours after. He'd gotten used to the quiet for so long that, now, noises above a normal conversation gave him headaches.

Soon Morty quieted down, as Bella May said nothing, just standing in front of him with her lantern and shears. Morty was panting heavily and snarling.

"Are you finished throwing your temper tantrum, young man?" she'd asked him calmly.

Morty reared his head back as far as he could and opened his mouth to start screaming again. It was so fast, Vern wasn't sure he saw it correctly. Bella May brought the poultry shears up and shot them into Morty's mouth and pulled them out just as quick. Instead of cursing, Morty had screamed in pain, blood flying out of his mouth, and then the blood was running down his chin and onto his chest.

It was like a horrific waterfall of blood that gushed forth from his mouth. His eyes were wild with fear and disbelief. He'd then stuck his tongue out, and Vern could see that she'd cut the tip of his tongue down the middle, forking it. Vern had felt lightheaded at the sight.

"Now, if I hear another word from you, I'll cut the rest of it off. Be glad I only clipped you, young man," Bella May had said, and, with a satisfied nod, she'd left the men alone in the dark.

Morty had moaned and cried for several hours after that but had eventually quieted down. He'd fallen asleep later, still shivering from the cold and the speed of her vengeance.

Vern heard the door open from above. He'd been thinking about it all night or all day, he wasn't sure, but he needed to tell her. He waited, and hoped as she came down the steps. He could smell something cooking from above as it wafted down the steps behind her.

When she got down to the landing, he could see that she was going to harvest some meat. He looked over to Morty, who looked like he'd bathed in a slaughterhouse. A shiver ran through him.

"Bella May?" Vern called softly. He watched as she turned to him.

"Yes Vern?"

"Can I talk to you for a minute?"

"Sure, Vern. What's on your mind?"

"Bella May, I want you to go ahead and kill me. Like you did for Hobo. I'm ready to die. I'm so tired of living, I don't even want you to set me free. Just let me go, Bella May. Please. You'll have plenty of me to can and use. Please, please just kill me," he asked, his voice soft. All the fight had left him a long time ago.

He looked into her green eyes, and he actually saw kindness there. He almost wanted to cry, and he hoped she would kill him.

143

"All right, Vern. Since you asked so nicely, I'll do it. And it won't hurt, Vern, I promise."

"I know. I saw it didn't hurt Hobo. Thanks, Bella May, really. Thank you."

He watched as she went over and set her things on the table. Morty was watching her, and Vern could see the abject fear in the man's eyes. Vern knew that fear very well. He'd worn it like a second skin, and was tired of it.

Vern was ready to die and looked forward to it. He didn't know what was on the other side, but it sure as hell had to be better than this. He was tired of being cold, being in pain, being in the dark. He knew he was on the precipice of madness, and he didn't want to go over it like Hobo had.

Bella May walked back over with her scalpel. She pulled out the bucket from beneath, and he could smell his own waste. But he didn't look down into it. He didn't want that to be the last thing he saw. He turned his face away from Bella May, giving her clear access to his neck. He felt the swift cut of the scalpel, and it didn't hurt. It almost felt like a nick from his razor when he shaved.

"Thanks, Bella May. It didn't hurt," he said. His eyes closed as he felt, with each heartbeat, the blood jetting from his neck. A soft smile curved his mouth. Breathing was becoming harder, but he didn't mind. Then his eyes shot open and he laughed.

"Well hello, Hobo, what the hell are you doing here?" Then his eyes closed slowly, and his head fell to his chest.

He was dead.

CHAPTER SEVEN

Mary sat up in bed. Her back pain had grown worse over the last few hours. It was early morning and she didn't want to disturb Jutta. The poor woman worked so hard, between taking care of her own family and taking care of Mary. She could see the dim light outside and the room was cold around her. Soft snores emanated from the other bed; the girls were sound asleep. Mary leaned forward and placed her hands on her back. She pushed in deep.

Then she felt a contraction, and her heart skipped a beat. Warm liquid leaked between her thighs. Hand trembling, she felt between her legs and swiped a finger, then looked at it in the muted light. She couldn't see anything and let her breath out. It wasn't blood. She shifted her hips and more fluid came out.

"My water's broken," she whispered softly. *It's too soon*, her mind cried. She got up from her bed and quietly made her way to Jutta's room. The warm liquid kept sliding down her thighs. She tapped lightly on the door, her hand shaking badly. Her lips trembled, and warm tears slid down her cheeks.

The door opened and Jutta's face, which quickly changed from sleepy to worried appeared. "Is everything okay, Mary?"

"I think my water's broke. It's too soon, Jutta," her voice cracked, and a sob slipped through her lips.

Jutta pulled her into an embrace, the strong arms encircling her. "Does the baby still move?"

"Yes, though he has slowed down. My back is hurting too," Mary said softly, her face buried in Jutta's neck.

"That is labor. We can't stop this, now that the water has broken. But it is good the baby moves. Go back to bed, I'll be in there soon. I want to go down stairs and get things ready. Don't worry. You're eight months, right?"

Mary pulled back and looked into Jutta's face, and nodded. She tried to smile but could not. Jutta patted her back and pushed her toward her room. She went back and got under the quilts. The room wasn't freezing, but it wasn't overly warm either. She pulled the quilts up to her chin and shook with fear. She hoped the baby would be okay. There was no hospital or emergency room.

There would be no incubator, no medicine for her child. She knew she was being foolish, but she wished David were there to hold her hand. He made her feel better, calm and safe. She knew it was absurd, since there was nothing he could do to help.

Jutta came in a few minutes later with an armload of towels and sheets, and placed them at the bottom of Mary's bed. Walking over to her

147

daughters, she shook them awake. As she murmured softly to the girls, they looked over to Mary with wide, frightened eyes. Then they both nodded, got up, and left the room. Mary could hear them going downstairs.

"They're going to make sure we have what we need. If you want, pull up your gown. I'll put these old sheets over and under you," Jutta said as she helped shift and move the linens around. She then placed several towels under Mary. Pulling the quilts back up, she tucked Mary back into bed. Because it was cold, Jutta rubbed her hands together quickly and blew on them.

"I'm going to feel around on your stomach. I'm sorry that my hands are cold." Lifting the quilts, she slid her hands beneath. Mary sucked in her breath as Jutta placed her chilled hands on Mary's distended abdomen, but her hands soon warmed, and Mary relaxed.

Both women felt the baby move beneath Jutta's hands, and Jutta grinned up at Mary. "I don't think we have to worry. The baby will be small, but I think he'll be healthy. You've been here well over a month, and we've been feeding the hell out of you," she said and grinned.

Mary grinned back, feeling a little better. She felt the woman's hands push and prod. The baby kicked back, and once more they smiled.

"You've dropped, for sure. And it feels like the baby has already headed down into the birth canal. It may be a few hours, or more. We'll time the contractions when they are stronger and closer together. Right now, it is a waiting game. Try to get some sleep. I'm going to go down and get a few things ready. Let me know if you see any blood," Jutta said, patting Mary on the knee.

Mary watched as Jutta left and shut the door behind her. Mary shifted, leaned over the bed and pulled out a box that had been placed there a few weeks ago. She and Jutta had gone through some old baby clothing. She set the box up on the bed beside her and opened it.

She pulled out a receiving blanket, a blue one. Her hand smoothed over the soft material. She next pulled out several cloth diapers, with duckling diaper pins attached. Then she pulled out a soft blue smock with a drawstring at the bottom. It was small, and she held the small garment to her and wept, fear and hope warring within her.

XXX

Jutta sat in the kitchen, drinking a cup of coffee. Her hands trembled. She'd delivered plenty of goats, colts, and other animals, but she'd never delivered a human baby. She had attended several births, but had not delivered, though her mother and grandmother had. She'd, of course, had her own children, but it was different on the other side of that equation. She took a deep breath and closed her eyes.

"You okay, Momma?" Milly asked.

"Yes. I'm just scared and nervous. Nature will take care of most of the baby's birth, but if there's an emergency, there's not much I can do. I've set out my herbs and started some water to steep teas if I need them. But still, I'd feel better if I had a doctor here," Jutta said with brutal honesty.

"Momma, you know you can do this. You take such good care of us, and you've delivered hundreds of farm animals over the years," Milly said, putting her arms around her mother.

Jutta's eyes teared up. When had her daughter become a woman? When had she grown up? She leaned back and looked into her daughter's blueberry eyes. There was sharp intelligence there, and a calmness. She wrapped her arm around her daughter and drew her into her lap, as she'd done so many years before. Cradling Milly, she kissed her bright head.

"I know you're right, honey. Thank you. Okay, let's get breakfast for everyone, and then get things ready for Mary. Hopefully it will be a smooth birth."

Jutta dug around in her dried herbs for blue cohosh and witch hazel. Those would be for postpartum bleeding. She didn't expect much, or rather she hoped for none, but one never knew. She'd rather have it ready and not need it, than need it and not have it ready. She had sterilized small scissors, needles, and thread. She wrapped these in clean gauze, ready for use. She took down a small bottle of mineral oil, in case she needed that to help ease the baby's head out of the canal. She didn't think she would, since the baby was early.

Then she watched as her children and husband came down for breakfast. She sent Milly up to check on Mary.

"Is she ready to have that baby then?" Gerhard asked his wife as he took in all her preparations. He kissed her on the cheek, and she felt his hand on her ample rump, patting it gently.

"Yes, her water's broken. We can't stop the baby from coming, and I think he'll be okay. She's only about five or six weeks from her delivery date. He'll be small, but we've fed her up this last month or so."

"I know you'll get that babe safely here. I'll make sure the boys get anything you need. Just give a shout if you need me," he said, and sat down at the table to eat his breakfast. Milly had made pancakes, hash browns, fried eggs, and fresh milk. Seth had already been out to milk the cows an hour earlier.

Once her things were assembled on her tray, Jutta went back up into the bedroom and lit a hurricane lantern. She then opened the curtains, letting the morning light in. Mary was dozing. *Good. She'll need her strength,* Jutta thought.

She left and went downstairs to eat her own breakfast. She saw that the children were cleaning up the breakfast dishes, and she smiled. She never had to tell them to do chores. They were a good bunch of kids and she was proud of them.

When the power had gone out, there hadn't been a whole lot that had changed. They'd grown up working hard: doing chores, taking care of the animals, taking care of each other. They all worked in the garden, and the boys with their father in the fields.

Though they no longer went to school, in the evening they sat working on assignments she'd put together. She didn't want ignorant children, even if the world had gone to hell. They had an extensive library, thanks to her mother and grandmother, who'd known the value in education and learning. There were also various books on nursing and biology.

Thinking hard, Jutta went to the office and pulled one of them down. Flipping through it, she found the section on childbirth and postpartum after care. She'd delivered many babies, animal babies, but again, she reminded herself, nature had a big hand in it all. She was only there to assist. Milly came into the home office and she looked up.

"Mary says the contractions are getting harder and closer together."

"All right," Jutta said, putting the book aside. "Go wash your hands and change into something clean, but old; it might get messy. I'll go change as well."

XXX

Boney and Wilber had waited all night, and dawn was approaching quickly. Both felt deflated. They'd lain in wait for Ralph Finch and his brother Aiden, having gotten word that the men lived in this house, but they'd spent all night waiting. They'd arrived at midnight and cased the house out. They had even gone so far as to enter. No one had been there.

"They're probably out drinkin' or something. We can wait," Boney had said. They'd settled themselves across the road, in an old roadside shed. Wilber had fallen asleep as Boney kept watch. Then Boney woke his friend up and took his turn to nap. Now they could both hear the morning birds, and light was pinkening the sky.

"I wonder where they is?" Wilber said, standing and stretching. He groaned heavily, joints popping.

"Ain't no telling. You gonna go see that grandson of yours?" Boney asked, taking a drink of water. They'd both brought food and water with them, unsure of how long they'd be.

"I will later tonight. I'll want to get proper sleep afore I go."

"It's a dang good thing that boy made it to the good doctor. I reckon God was watching," Boney said and smiled kindly.

"You wanna just leave and try again?" Wilber asked, disappointment clear in his voice.

Boney was about to say yes, when they heard a man's laughter. Both men froze. Boney stood, looking out between the slotted cracks of the dilapidated building.

Down the road, two men staggered toward them. It was the Finch brothers. Looked like they were still drunk, Ralph carrying what looked like a bottle, a few ounces of the amber booze sloshing around in the bottom. Aiden had said something that had made Ralph laugh, and then crudely grab his crotch. Both nearly fell to the road in laughter.

Boney smiled. This would be like shooting fish in a barrel. They waited as both men drew closer. He and Wilber could now make out their disturbing conversation.

"That gal kept sayin' no, but I kept shutting her up," Ralph laughed hard, and then grabbed his crotch again.

"I seen it, brother. Those sisters was ripe for the taking, I'll swear," Aiden laughed coarsely.

154

"That bitch of a mother should have just kept her mouth shut. I'd not have to have stoved her head in otherwise."

"Yeah, that did kinda ruin the mood," Aiden agreed, grabbing the bottle of liquor from his brother and taking a long swig.

Boney had heard enough. He nudged Wilber, then looked at him. Both men lifted their guns. It would be loud as hell in that small structure.

"You wanna just step out and shoot 'em?" Boney said. There were no other houses around, and their truck was well hidden down the road. It would beat having their eardrums blown.

"Sure. I want these little bastards to see it coming," Wilber said.

Boney grinned at his friend and patted him on the back. They went out of the structure from the back, and stepped out in the road, weapons raised. The men were about fifteen feet away and hadn't noticed them yet. Boney cleared his throat.

The two men stopped, looked up, and the smiles on their faces evaporated.

"Who the hell are you?" Ralph said belligerently.

"Not that it's any of your business, but you can call me Death." Boney laughed, and saw the realization dawn on Ralph's face that he was indeed death.

155

Aiden dropped the bottle and looked as though he were trying to dig his weapon out from his waistband. Ralph was doing the same. Boney and Wilber shot nearly simultaneously, the sound echoing off the hills around them. The birds stopped their singing, and as the echo faded and the smoke cleared, and the dust settled, the brothers lay dead in the road.

Boney walked over, Wilber beside him, his head on a swivel, looking around. There was neither movement nor sound from anywhere. Boney kicked at Ralph's foot. He then leaned over and pulled out the gun; a Glock. *Too nice a weapon for this peckerhead*, he thought.

"I'll make sure one of them folks from the coal mine get this weapon." He lifted the weapon and grinned at Wilber.

"That's a nice one. This one had a .38 snub," Wilber said.

"Let's go home, friend, and get some sleep. These two assholes won't be bothering any more sisters or mothers," Boney said, and both men walked down the deserted road, the birds beginning their morning songs once more.

XXX

Mary grunted and lay back in the bed, her face red and pale by turns. Milly took a small towel and patted her face. Mary turned and smiled at the girl.

156

The pains were now nearly unbearable. She panted, trying to catch her breath. It had been three hours and still the baby hadn't come. The pain was now just about nonstop. She had but a few moments reprieve between when the contractions started again, her uterus contracting, like a fist, clenched and hard.

Jutta had checked her and said it could be anytime now.

"Pant in slow, short breaths, Mary. Try to concentrate on that and try to relax the rest of your body. You're so close now," Jutta said encouragingly, a smile on her face.

Mary could hear activity outside and down below in the house. She heard laughter. It sounded like a normal day in a normal life. Somehow, that made her feel better. She panted just as Jutta had told her.

"I feel like I need to push," she said suddenly.

"Good. Then push, Mary. Milly, get behind Mary and support her," Jutta ordered calmly.

Milly got behind Mary and placed her warm hands on Mary's shoulders. Mary sat up and shifted forward, her knees drawn up, hands holding on to them. She grunted and pushed.

"Push, push, push," Jutta repeated like a mantra. Mary pushed for as long as she could. Jutta checked her and grinned up at Mary.

"He's crowning," she said, and got the small bottle of mineral oil and put some on her fingers. Reaching down, she applied it to Mary.

Mary was panting again, the color fading from her face. She tried to smile, but the pain was so great. It was like nothing she'd ever experienced before. It was as though her guts were being ripped from her. The wave of pain began once more. She leaned back and felt Milly's steadying hands behind her. Mary grabbed her knees and pushed once more.

"Stop! His head is out. Let me turn him." There was silence as Jutta worked. "The cord is clear. Okay, you can push now," Jutta commanded like a drill sergeant.

Mary watched as Jutta guided the baby out, moving the small shoulders and letting the baby glide from her. The pain was now gone, replaced by her son there, so tiny. He was nearly a purplish blue, and fear skittered through her.

She was paralyzed as she watched Jutta take the thread and tie it around the umbilical cord; her hands were sure and fast. Then she saw the small scissors and watched as Jutta cut the cord above the tied string.

She tried to talk, but her mouth was dry. So instead, she watched the woman take her son in her large capable hands. Jutta wrapped the baby in a towel and began to pat his back, his small head facing down. Liquid came from the baby's mouth and Jutta continued to pat and rub him. Then he jerked, and a tiny wail came out. Mary could breathe again.

The tiny, froglike legs kicked, the toes spread, and small arms waved angrily. The baby sucked in a breath and let out an even louder shriek, his small face purple and red now, his tiny fists shaking with indignant rage. Both women laughed and looked at each other. Milly got up and retrieved the receiving blanket. Jutta wrapped the baby up snug, then handed him over to Mary.

"Here is your son, Mary. He's tiny, but he's a fighter," Jutta said, tears sliding down her face, a huge smile on her face.

"Oh, Jutta, he's beautiful, and my God, so tiny. Hello Howard David Deets! How are you, my son?" Mary cooed.

She held Howard up and looked into his dark, bluish eyes. His hair was jet black and his body was still covered with vernix and tiny hairs. His small eyes blinked in confusion, and Mary laughed. His small mouth looked like a tiny rosebud. She kissed him and sniffed him. He was hers, and he was here.

She felt Jutta working below her, then watched as the woman left the room. Milly sat down beside her and looked at the baby.

"He's so small, Miss Mary, but he sure is beautiful," she said wistfully.

"He is. I can't believe how perfect he is!" Mary said, her eyes transfixed on the tiny form in her arms.

Jutta came back in, a huge smile on her face. She bustled around the room, straightening it up.

"Milly, go make Mary some lunch. Something light, and get her some milk too."

"Yes ma'am," Milly said. She grinned at Mary and kissed her cheek. Then she kissed the top of the baby's head gently and disappeared from the room.

"I'd say he weighs about five pounds. That isn't too bad, Mary. He's a preemie, but he's a good size. I think if you'd taken him to term, he'd have been a nine-pounder," Jutta laughed.

"Oh my, that would hurt like hell, I don't even want to imagine what a nine-pounder feels like," Mary said and laughed.

"It sure as hell don't feel good. Three of mine were nine pounds, the others seven or eight," Jutta said, shaking her head.

Mary looked at her and shook her head. Then she looked down at Howard and grinned.

"In a little while," Jutta went on, "I'm going to come back and knead your stomach. It'll hurt, but it will help your uterus shrink down to size. Did you want to try to nurse him? See if he'll latch?"

"Yes, I'd like that," Mary said, and let Jutta help pull her gown down enough for her breast to come out. Jutta showed her how to knead and push the colostrum out, the important first milk. Mary placed the baby to her breast and enticed the baby to take the nipple. Howard latched on with alacrity. Mary laughed, and watched in awe as her son took his first drink.

XXX

Wilber drove slowly toward Harry's old farmhouse. It was dusk, and all was quiet on the road. He and Boney had gone their separate ways that morning, and he'd gone to bed for a good long rest. He'd not been so active for years, and he felt young once more. It was a good feeling. He hoped, however, that this conflict would end soon, before Alan was killed.

To see his grandson so fragile nearly broke his old heart. No child should have to see what his grandson had seen, or be shot at by a couple of booger-eaters. He was glad Harry had taken care of it, and he was glad Alan would have Harry and his family once he passed on. He had no plans for now but knew Alan wouldn't be alone after he was gone. That was good.

His headlights led the way to the large farmhouse on the hill. Ahead, he saw eyes of deer, standing just inside the tree line. Once Alan was better, they'd go hunting. It was about time. The rut would start in a few short weeks. He pulled up the road a bit past the barricade, which had grown in nicely over the past few months. He clicked on his old flashlight and walked to the barricade.

A flashlight worked its way down the hill. Someone was coming to meet him. Harry, he figured. He smiled up at the younger man as he drew near, and patted him on his shoulders.

"How is it, Harry? How's my grandson?"

"He's doing really good. Has been eating solid food and enjoying all the attention the women are giving him," Harry said and chuckled.

"Yeah, he always did like being petted," Wilber said, smiling.

"Willene said you're staying for dinner and you're staying for the night. She already has your room made up for you. We'd like it if you stayed with us while Alan is here. It also gives us a chance to plan out our strategies for Friday."

Wilber nodded, and grinned.

They reached the porch, which was dark, but he could make out the shapes of the people sitting there.

"Hi, Wilber, how are you this evening?" Clay asked.

"I'm good, son. Boney sends his best."

"Alight then," Clay said, nodding.

"I'll fetch you some dinner, Wilber. Have a seat," Willene ordered.

"Where's Earl?" Wilber asked, looking around.

"He's on watch. He's making a round on the property, but should be back in a bit," Marilyn chimed in. They all turned their heads as Willene came to the door. Monroe opened it for her and grinned up at her. It sure felt like a home here, and Wilber was glad Alan was here. He was in capable hands.

Marilyn got up and set a TV tray in front of Wilber. Then Willene set a plate of fried chicken, mashed potatoes, corn on the cob, with some sliced tomatoes, and a glass of sun tea down on it.

Wilber picked the glass up to take a drink and was gratified to note that it was cold.

"This sure does look good, thank ya, gals." He grinned and began to dig in. Then stopped, realizing he'd not even gone in to see his grandson.

"Oh shoot, I guess I should check on my grandson first," he said in embarrassment.

"It's okay. He's asleep right now. Go ahead and eat, Wilber. He'll bide," Katie said, she was sitting with Clay.

He nodded, then dug into the food. Marilyn sat back down beside Harry, and pulled Monroe into her lap. They all sat quietly as Wilber ate, enjoying the cool evening. They could hear the dogs in the woods with Earl, and a chuckle ran through the group as they heard Earl talking to the dogs.

"Boney and me bagged us a couple of idgits this mornin'. Was afraid we might not get any, but

163

we did. Got the two Finch brothers, Ralph and Aiden," Wilber said.

"Them some bad'ens," Boggy said from the side of the porch.

"Yes, they are or should I say, was," Wilber agreed.

"I've arrested both those boys on domestic disturbances several times. Unfortunately, the women involved didn't press charges," Clay said.

"Well, now they're no longer a goin' concern," Wilber said laughing, and everyone joined in.

"I can't say I agree with all the killing and violence, but I tended to those women, so I really can't be sorry that those brutes are gone," Katie said.

"Don't you cry no tears for these idgits, Doc. They done had choices in this life. They just chose wrong. And now they'd paid for it," Wilber said, his voice sober.

"Have you any ideas for Friday, after we free the prisoners from the coal mine?" Harry asked.

"I think we separate into three teams. Darkness will be our friend. Me an' you and Boggy will go to the Bluemont Bed an' Breakfast. Boggy takes the TNT if we need it, but hoping we don't," Wilber said, nodding his head to Boggy.

"I figure Clay'll want to take care of Yates, but if you want to take someone as back up, I reckon

Ralph and Abram will enjoy goin' with you," Wilber cackled.

"Sure. I don't think I'll need back up, but I don't know if Yates will have men with him or helping to guard him. I'll also take Earl. Once I take care of him, we can join you, Harry, and Boggy," Clay said softy.

"Good. Boney an' Sherman will hunt down stragglers. Reece Archer and Murphy Tweet is the last of the klavern, and anyone who is hangin' with them, they're gonna die too," Wilber said.

"Will you spare anyone who surrenders?" Katie asked. Everyone waited for Wilber to answer, and the creaks of the swing and glider filled the void.

"No, we give no quarter. They done killed children; they put children in that coal mine. No, they all die. They was gonna kill you, Katie, as they killed your momma. We kill them all, otherwise they'll try to raise up again later. I don't want my grandson living in a world where he's gotta watch his back 'cause we didn't finish the job," Wilber explained, his voice hard and determined.

"I agree. They deserve no more than a bullet to the brain," Clay said.

"I agree too," Boggy said softly, and Wilber could hear the rage.

"Yeah," Harry said. "We can't afford to let any of them live. For our children's sakes." He patted

Monroe's head; the boy was asleep in his mother's arms.

"Depending on who can help from the coal mine, we'll be split between us. I don't want Gerhard mixed in with this. His family needs him, as does his community," Wilber said.

Everyone grunted agreement, and he smiled. He'd thought they would. He sat back, finished with his dinner. It had been a fine spread, and he'd enjoyed it immensely.

"I'm gonna go see my grandson, then I'm headin' ta bed. It's been a long day for sure. Thank ya ladies for a fine meal. I appreciate it," Wilber said, getting up stiffly.

Willene joined him, picking up his tray and leading the way into the house. The occupants on the porch watched Willene lead the older man away. It truly was a miracle that Alan had made it there and survived.

CHAPTER EIGHT

Mary held her son, his small soft head cradled in her hand. Her lips glided over the soft fuzz that had sprung up from Howard's tiny head. She inhaled the magical, antediluvian fragrance of him. She wondered if the enticing scent bound her to him, bonded her irrevocably to this child? For certain, she was linked to him, body and soul. The soft feel of his body, his boneless weight filling her arms and her heart. He'd fed well, and she lifted his miniature hand with her finger. It amazed her how tiny the nails were.

Leaning her head down, she kissed the small hand and fingers. She was hopelessly in love. From below, she heard activity and laughter. She smiled. At some point, she would have to leave this home, and she would be bereft. It had been not only a sanctuary but a place of love and friendship. She thought of her friendship with David. She wasn't a fool; she'd seen the love in his eyes. He was a good man, and she cared deeply for him.

She loved her husband, and knew Howard wouldn't be angry at her for caring about David. She looked out the window. It was getting dark. In a couple days, the people, her friends, would try to take their town back. She'd heard all the talking below, and Jutta had told her of the plan. Soon.

167

She heard Jutta coming up the stairs, and she saw Milly behind her, carrying an oil lamp. Jutta came in with a tray of food, and Milly put the lamp on the nightstand. She then took the tray from her mother and Jutta reached for the baby, a gentle smile caressing her face.

"Let me have that little boy. Oh, I miss having a little little. They always smell so darn good and so very sweet," she said, lifting the small bundle gently. She brought the baby up to her face, and sniffed and kissed the small head tenderly, smiling and cooing.

Milly placed the tray on Mary's lap and grinned shyly, then left the room. Mary inhaled. The food smelled wonderful, and she was hungry.

"Thank you so much for taking care of us both, Jutta. I really appreciate it," Mary said, and took a bite of baked chicken, fried squash, mashed sweet potatoes, green beans, and sliced tomatoes. Her eyes closed in heavenly delight. Jutta could cook.

"Oh, honey, you are a treasure, and now we have a new jewel. He's so beautiful, it just breaks my heart, I'll swear," Jutta said, her voice cracking with emotion.

Mary smiled, and she felt her eyes sting with tears. In a time so hateful and dangerous, she'd found a new family who loved her, and she loved them back.

"I almost hate to leave once this is over," Mary said, taking a drink of milk.

"But you don't have to, you know, Mary. You are welcome to stay with us," Jutta said earnestly as she gently patted the baby's back in a rhythmic fashion.

"I know, and I may well be here for a while, but I'm hoping that I can find a home near here, maybe. I know there are abandoned homes. I'd go back to my own if they'd not burned it down," she said sadly.

"Let me talk to Gerhard, I'll have him look around. I think there is a small place right up the road. The family who lived there was away on vacation. They'd gone down to Disney World. I don't think they'll be back, God love 'em."

"Oh, that would be wonderful," Mary said, thrilled. She'd be close enough to walk and see her friends here.

Jutta got up and walked to the door. She called her husband, then came and sat back down beside Mary's bed. "I don't think I could let you or this little one get too far from me," she said and grinned.

Gerhard stuck his head into the room. He grinned at Mary and ducked his head shyly, then came in and looked down at Howard. His mouth made a soundless oh, and he looked at Mary with unconcealed delight. "Can I hold him?" he asked, his voice awed, and at Mary's nod, he took the baby with infinite care.

"Oh, for the love of God, he's beautiful, Mary. He's so tiny, and such a miracle," he said thickly.

Mary smiled. She knew she couldn't be far from this family. She'd fallen in love with them all.

"Honey, can you go check out the Bilford's house? And take the boys with you. Mary will need a home to live in with her new little family. I want her close to us."

"Oh Mary, you ain't leavin' us so soon, are you?" Gerhard asked, clearly distressed. He almost clutched the baby to his chest.

Jutta laughed softly and shook her head. "No, silly man, but she will need her own home one of these days. When she's ready, I want it ready for her."

"Thank you, Gerhard," Mary said and smiled softly.

Gerhard grinned and nodded, kissing the baby's head and handing the small bundle, carefully if reluctantly, back to his wife. He then kissed the top of her bright head and left the room.

"I'll swear, that man is a handful," Jutta laughed.

"Yes, but he's your handful, and he clearly loves you very much," Mary said. She was enjoying her dinner and the company. It was a busy house, and she would be glad when she could get up and around easier.

"He is that. I think the men will be making their move day after tomorrow. Boney and Wilber have stopped by and had a talk with Gerhard. They are going to free everyone from the mines."

"I hope it won't be too dangerous. I know the people in the mine are weakened from lack of food. Where will they all go?" Mary worried aloud.

"From what I understand, they found a large cache of food and supplies. Boney and Wilber, and some other men, will go and collect it. They'll parcel it out among the families, and we're also going to send them food. There are their own extended families that will take them, and others have volunteered to take them until they can take care of themselves. More than likely until next summer, when they have their own gardens," Jutta explained.

"It will be hard, but I do think that, once they are free and can hunt and do for themselves, they'll be okay," Mary hoped.

"I expect you're right. There've been a lot of good folks killed, and a lot have died. Gerhard thinks that our population has gone down by better than half," Jutta said sadly.

"Good Lord, that's terrible. What happened to the food you sent to the mayor?"

EMP Antediluvian Courage   S.A. Ison

"I don't know. The bastard more than likely used it solely for himself and his horrible people. Boney said that some of the places around town stink. I don't know if those places will ever be inhabitable."

"Oh, for the love of God. What a terrible time. I hope we can recover from this. I hope there are enough good people left," Mary said, sorrow filling her heart.

"As long as we have a few, we have enough. I know there are families in the hills, hunkered down. There's us, David, the folks from the coal mine and others. We'll make it, I'm sure. We just need to get rid of the bad 'uns."

"I expect this will have taught the remaining townspeople to appreciate each other. Maybe work hard to keep things humane, and work together to help one another," Mary said softly.

"You don't have to worry, Mary. We'll take care of you and you'll take care of us. You're our family now. We've already adopted you and Howard," Jutta said and beamed.

XXX

Harry stood on the porch, looking out over the valley. There was a thick fog below that covered the mountains around them. It was just getting light, and the air was hushed and cold. His breath fogged before him. In the distance, he heard a dog baying.

172

Brian, Homer, and Charlie were in the yard, sniffing around. Surprisingly, they all got along. He watched as they disappeared into the tree line. The porch door opened, and he smiled at Clay, who also had a cup of coffee.

"Mornin'. Sleep good?" Clay asked.

"Like a baby," Harry said.

"I'm going to ask Katie to marry me today," Clay said without preamble.

"I was wondering when you'd get around to that," Harry said and chuckled.

"I'd like to have some kind of ceremony later today. Maybe Willene can make a cake or something. There isn't a preacher, but I figure if it is done with friends and family and God, then it is legal and official," Clay said, though Harry heard the note of worry in his voice.

"I'd say you're right about that. I'll talk to Willene and see if we can't surprise Katie with something special."

"I just hope tomorrow goes without a hitch. I'd like to live in this world without the worry of assholes like that floating around our town," Clay said.

"I hope so too. We just need to keep frosty and make sure we get it done right the first time. Keep casualties to zero."

The porch door opened, and Wilber walked out smiling, a cup of coffee and a biscuit in hand.

"Mornin', boys," he said, his voice like gravel, heavy with sleep.

"Mornin'," both men said simultaneously.

"A little cool this morning, makes for fine sleepin'," Wilber chuckled.

"It sure does. Makes it hard to get out of bed," Clay laughed ruefully.

"I'm going to go talk to Willene, then I think I'll head down to Joshua's and talk to him," Harry said, and left the two men to their coffee.

He walked into the kitchen. Boggy and Earl were sitting at the table, both with a biscuit and fried egg. He grinned at them. Marilyn was sitting with Monroe, who was sleepily nibbling on his own biscuit. He reached over and grasped the child's head, eliciting a giggle that threw crumbs across the table. Harry grinned and winked at Marilyn.

Katie was on patrol and would be in shortly. He'd have to tell everyone and get down to Joshua's.

"Clay is going to ask Katie to marry him. He wants to do it today and he wants to know if you can make her a surprise wedding cake?"

The kitchen erupted with laugher and surprised gasps. They all talked at once, the excitement shifting their sleepy faces to happy and alert. Angela was still upstairs, asleep in her crib. They'd found the old crib out in the barn and he and Boggy had cleaned it up. It was good for keeping the child in bed while Willene cooked breakfast.

"Oh, I think we can manage a cake. We'll need some more milk and butter, though," Willene said, her eyes distant in thought.

"I figured you might. I'm heading down to Joshua's, so I'll pick some up. I'll take him a bushel of walnuts for trade," Harry said, grabbing an egg-filled biscuit. He bit in, and it was wonderful. Willene was now using the wood cook stove in the kitchen, and it heated the house up nicely. Especially the room over the kitchen.

"I'll see if I can find some pretty flowers later, as soon as this fog lifts," Marilyn said.

"Doesn't Joshua play the fiddle? I think he might," Willene asked.

"He sure do. He played at the fair last year. Was real good, too," Earl put in.

"See if he and Pauline will come for the wedding, say about four this afternoon, and maybe he can play some music and we'll make a nice party of it," Willene suggested, grinning.

The back door opened, and Katie stepped in. She was bundled in a large jacket and cap. Everyone stopped talking all at once and looked pointedly at her. She stopped and looked at everyone.

"What?" she asked.

The room erupted in laughter and sniggers, and no one said a thing. Clay walked in and saw Katie, and grinned. Harry laughed at Katie's confusion. Wilber came in and bumped into Clay, who stumbled forward. Then Clay walked over to Katie and got down on his knee. The room grew immediately quiet, everyone hushing the other. Katie looked at the people around her, and then down at Clay, who was looking up at her with earnest eyes. Harry's chest clutched, his heart nearly breaking.

Katie's eyes filled with tears, a huge smile on her face.

"Katie, would you do me the honor of becoming my wife?"

Katie lunged forward and wrapped her arms around Clay's neck, and Harry heard her muffled, "Yes".

The room erupted in shouts of congratulations and back patting and hugs and laughter. Katie was crying, as were Willene and Marilyn. He too felt choked up, and grinned. Clay was grinning like a loon, and tears streaked down his face. Harry shook his head. It was amazing the joy in this house, even under these difficult times. He felt blessed and thankful that he'd been here when all things went to hell. He could not imagine if he'd not been.

Willene left the kitchen; they could hear Angela calling for her momma. Monroe crawled across and sat with Earl, who tickled the little boy's neck with his finger. Marilyn laughed and put her hand around Earl's neck and drew him to her and kissed him on the cheek. Earl blushed and shrugged his shoulders up to his ears. Harry laughed. The room was loud and filled with laughter and crosstalk. It was truly a wonderful moment.

XXX

Harry and Boggy drove the short distance to the dairy and took the driveway that wound five hundred feet back from the road. The sun was trying to burn through the heavy fog. Though they could not see them, they heard the cows, their low calls rolling over the wet grass.

Boggy held a large basked filled with the black walnuts Monroe had collected. When they got near the barricade, one of Joshua's people halted the truck, then, recognizing Harry, waved him through.

Pauline Kinkade came out of the large two-story farmhouse. She had a red gingham towel over her shoulder and wore a yellow gingham apron. She lifted her hand in greeting and smiled as Harry pulled the truck near her.

"Good morning, Pauline. How are you doing?" Harry asked.

"I'm good, busy as ever. You lookin' for Joshua?"

"Sure am. Got a wedding today. Dr. Katie and Clay are getting married up at the house. You and Joshua are invited, along with his fiddle, of course," he said and smiled.

Pauline threw her head back and laughed. Then she shook her head, a wide smile on her face.

"I'll let him know. I wondered when those two would make it serious. They been dating off and on for years. What time should we be there?" she asked.

"About four. I need to do some trading, got a bushel of black walnuts for some milk and butter, if you have some to spare."

"I think we can accommodate. Who's your young friend?" she asked.

"Oh, I'm sorry, Pauline, this is Boggy Hines, Boggy, this is Pauline Kinkade," Harry said.

Boggy smiled shyly and waved. She smiled back and winked at him.

"I knew your granny, Boggy. A wonderful woman. Come on in, I'll get you some coffee ta warm ya up. It's a bit chilly. Then I'll go fetch the butter and milk for you." She turned back into the house.

Harry and Boggy got out of the truck. They kicked the dirt off their shoes before they went into the house. The smell of baking bread filled the house and wrapped its enticing tendrils around the two men.

"That sure does smell good," Boggy said softly, looking around the living room. The men walked into the kitchen and sat at a round, wooden table with a yellow tablecloth. Boggy set the basket of nuts onto the table and Pauline thanked him, and handed him a cup of coffee. She turned and gave another to Harry, then cut two large slices of apple pie and handed them to the men. Boggy's eyes widened in pleasure.

"You boys sit down and enjoy it. I'll go fetch Josh."

Harry and Boggy sat at the table and began to eat.

"I'm so glad I came with you. This here is some good pie." Boggy groaned in pleasure, his eyes closed and body rocking from side to side.

"Yeah. This is some fine pie at that. It goes well with this coffee," Harry agreed. The kitchen door opened, and Joshua and Pauline came in. Pauline carried a small crock of butter and Joshua two gallons of milk.

"How you men doin'?" Joshua asked.

"Good. Pauline, this is the best apple pie I've ever had. Don't tell Willene; she'll skin me alive," Harry said laughing.

Pauline smacked his shoulder lightly, in a good-natured gesture.

"Pauline said Clay finally popped the question to Katie. About time. We'll be there about four, and I'll rosin up my bow," Joshua said.

"Thanks, Josh. I also wanted to let you know, tomorrow, me and some men will be trying to free up the prisoners in the coal mine."

"Be careful. Yates and his men are no one to fool around with. What will become of all those people?" Joshua asked.

"We know they're a bad bunch. Friends of ours have been picking them off. Softening them up. Heard that Yates killed Audrey, so at least we don't need to worry about him," Harry said.

Joshua laughed and shook his head. "Yeah, that worthless fool needed killin'. Once you get them out and settled, I'll get milk, cheese, and butter ready for them. It won't be much, but it'll help."

"Thanks, Josh. We'll get out of your hair, as Willy wants to make a surprise wedding cake. See you at four."

Harry and Boggy left, carrying their prizes. It only took a few short minutes to get back to the house. Willene met them on the porch with a big smile.

"You can put the butter and one of those gallon jugs in the basement. I have a pan of well water down there that will keep it chilled," Willene instructed Boggy.

She took the other jug and went into the kitchen. Marilyn was there. Harry looked around; there was food everywhere, and when he reached for an apple, he got his hand smacked.

"Out," Willene ordered, causing Marilyn to laugh.

Harry looked at her, wounded, then turned and left the kitchen, their laughter following him. He stopped in the living room. Alan was sitting up and eating oatmeal. He grinned up at Harry.

"How ya feeling, Alan?"

"Fair ta middlin'. I reckon I'll survive," he said and grinned.

"You want to go out to the porch to sit? It's cool, but it's nice out there."

"Heck yeah, Harry, I'm tired of being cooped up," Alan said, throwing the blanket off. Harry walked over, just as Boggy was coming up from the basement. Boggy got on one side, Harry on the other, and they helped the teenager out to the porch. They set him in a rocking chair and Boggy went in to retrieve the quilt. He came out and tucked it around Alan.

Clay and Katie were in the glider, Wilber in another rocking chair. Earl was coming out from the tree line and lifted a hand. Harry and Boggy sat in the swing.

"Got kicked out too?" Clay grinned.

"Yeah. No respect in this house," Harry said.

"Don't feel bad. We've all been banished to the porch." Monroe and Angela were sitting on the porch, playing with blocks. Both were bundled up in coats and sweaters. The sun was burning through the haze and warming up the porch.

"Josh says he'll donate butter, milk, and cheese to the folks coming out of the coal mine, once they get settled," Harry announced.

"Oh, how wonderful. That is so kind of them," Katie said.

"Once everything is settled, I'll see what we can contribute. Hopefully they'll have enough to get them through the winter and into the spring and summer. It will be a lean winter," Harry said.

"I just hope them folks out there are huntin' an' foraging. There are a lot of nut trees an' apple trees out there. I hope they ain't waiting for others to do it for them," Wilber said. He was now trying to light his pipe, as the humidity was low enough to allow it.

"I have a feeling that those people have already died out. If they weren't willing to take care of themselves after all this time, I think they would have already starved to death," Harry said.

"That's true enough," Earl agreed. He stood at the edge of the porch, looking out and around. Harry noticed that he took out his pipe and lit it. He grinned.

"Hopefully it will go smoothly tomorrow. By tomorrow night, we'll have hunted the last of them down," Harry said.

"It seems like a lifetime has passed," Katie said, and Clay put his arm around her and hugged her to him.

"Well, one lifetime, I reckon, now a different life time. Now we're in the new," Boggy said quietly.

"Hopefully, we'll be in a better one. Hopefully, once this is done, we'll be able to go on with our lives, and though it will be simpler, hopefully it will be good," Harry said.

"Getting rid of the bad element will go a long way in ensuring that. I plan to make sure that it doesn't even try to raise its ugly head again in town," Clay said, hard resolve in his voice.

"I suspect that we'll be heading back to the way law used to be. No plea bargaining, no stays of executions," Harry said.

"I'm glad. They're a lot of bad people that got away with bad things, 'cause they got good lawyers. That wasn't right," Boggy said.

"No, but that was the way it was. But don't worry. I suspect people will be busy trying to survive to be out causing mischief. We are heading back to a time where there wasn't a whole lot of free time," Clay said.

"I'd say we're already there," Wilber laughed.

183

XXX

Joshua played the wedding song on his fiddle. It was high and sweet. Harry walked Katie out to the porch, where everyone had assembled. Willene had found their mother's wedding dress in the attic. She had sent Harry out to shake it and air it out. It had been well preserved, and in the damp air, the wrinkles had mostly come out. Katie was now dressed in it and she looked radiant. Marilyn had found some mums and made a small bouquet.

The dress was a little big, but the women had pinned it tight. Clay stood stiff in his uniform, his face a mask of nerves, love and fear. When he saw Katie, his eyes filled with tears and the tears slid silently down his face. Willene had put Angela to bed for a nap earlier, and they all knew she'd be up in a bit. They didn't need to rush, but Harry figured the fiddle would wake her soon.

Katie went to stand beside Clay, while Boggy came up with a Bible. They'd all agreed that Boggy should do the ceremony.

"Beloved friends and family. We are here to witness a marriage between two people whose lives have touched us all. We is blessed to know them and to share their lives. We are honored to help them join in holy wedlock." Boggy swallowed nervously, and a shy smile trembled on his lips.

"I ain't no preacher, but I guess God knows your true love and intention to each other. We sure seen it," he said, and there were soft giggles among the group.

"We've had trouble, but more than that, we've had the love an' keeping of each other. Now, you Clay, an' you Katie, will have the keepin' of each other. Let the Lord Jesus Christ bear witness, as do we, to this union. Clayton Patterson, do you take Katherine Lee to be your wife? Ta honor her and love her till you're dead?"

Clay's lips trembled, and Harry wasn't sure if it was nerves or a laugh at the way Boggy said the vows, but he had to bite the inside of his own cheek. He'd give Boggy credit; the man was a poet.

"I do," Clay answered in a low serious voice.

"Katherine Lee, do you take Clayton Patterson ta be your husband? Ta honor and love him till you're dead?"

"I do," she said, her smile radiant with joy and love.

"Though I don't have any legal standin', we are all witnesses here afore God, and God knows that you two love each other. I asked that you jump the broom, and then I pronounce you husband an' wife," Boggy said, and stepped back and laid down a broom. Clay grasped Katie's hand and they both jumped the broom. Joshua erupted in a song, *I am a Man of Constant Sorrow*, on his fiddle, and

185

everyone shouted and laughed. Clay picked up Katie and swung her around and kissed her.

Willene disappeared into the house and, a little later, brought a sleepy Angela out. She bounced the child on her hip to the rhythm of the music. Josh broke into different songs and everyone pushed back the rocking chairs and began to dance on the porch. He played *Rocky Top*, *Blue Moon of Kentucky*, and *Wayfaring Stranger* before he took a break.

Willene handed Angela off to Harry and disappeared into the house. She came out holding a sheet cake, and Marilyn opened the door for her. Katie turned around, saw the wedding cake, and began to cry anew. Faces lit with smiles and nods of approval. They all gathered round, and Katie and Clay took the knife, which had a strip of ribbon tied around it. Then they took a small piece and fed each other. The crowd applauded and laughed. Charlie, Brian, and Homer barked excitedly, though they were shooed off the porch.

Boggy brought out a pitcher of tea, and everyone settled to eat wedding cake and tea. Katie sat in Clay's lap so Pauline and Josh could sit beside them on the glider.

"This is wonderful cake, Willy. Thank you so much for making it," Katie said. There was a round of hmmms, and Willene laughed.

"It's our mother's recipe. Thanks."

"I thought it tasted familiar. I've not had this in years," Harry said.

"It sure is good. I could have another if that's okay?" Alan asked, his large eyes hopeful.

Willene laughed and cut a large piece for Alan and deposited it on his plate. "Don't get too filled up. We have a nice wedding supper too," she admonished him.

"Yes'm," he said, the side of his cheek bulging with cake.

Monroe jumped down and ran out into the yard to play with the dogs. Joshua tuned his fiddle and began to play once more, though it was a slower, softer tune.

Harry turned to Marilyn. "May I have this dance?" he grinned.

Marilyn blushed and nodded. He held out his hand and pulled her into his arms. As they danced, Earl pulled Willene out and danced with her, Angela between them. They laughed and twirled awkwardly about the porch. Finally, Katie and Clay joined in.

The day was nice, like an Indian Summer; the sun was bright and the sky a brilliant cerulean blue. A breeze was blowing from the northeast, moving the leaves softly. The food was set out on the kitchen table and the counters. The group brought their food to the porch to enjoy Burgoo, a venison dish with vegetables, corn pudding, fried okra,

187

green beans with a little pork, and sliced tomatoes. Everyone settled down to some serious eating and the group quieted down.

"I'll tell ya, this is some fine eatin'," Wilber said, wiping his mouth with a napkin.

"It sure is. Can you adopt me, Willy?" Alan asked, his face turning bright red.

Willene laughed and shook her head. Harry thought it was good, and he was glad he could share it with his friends.

CHAPTER NINE

David, Gideon, and Steven waited their turn to get on the bus. Each man knew this was their last day, and hopefully their families' last day, in the coal mine. Each man's head was down, as though subdued. It wouldn't do for the two guards to see the glitter of suppressed rage and excitement in their eyes. Their body language echoed their cowed posture. There were eleven of them.

For David, it was also suppressing his desire to see Mary. It had been nearly two and a half weeks, and his thoughts had been filled with worry for her. Had she lost the baby? His heart fluttered uncomfortably in his chest. It had torn him to pieces, having to leave her, but there wasn't much he could do. He would have indeed been missed had he not returned to the mine.

She'd felt so frail and light in his arms when he'd carried her up. He knew that had she not have left the coal mine when she did, the baby would have died. And, his heart squeezed hard, *may well be dead*, he thought. If the baby had died, Mary would be devastated. It was her last link to Howard, and it'd been her hope and her joy. He'd prayed daily, if not hourly, for the baby to survive.

The not knowing was the worst. Having to leave her had damned near killed him. But he couldn't risk her safety, or that of the Friedhof family. It would have been poor payback for their kindness and generosity. He moved to the back of the bus and looked out at the dim morning. The clouds were low lying, and he could smell the petrichor, the indescribable ozone scent that heralds the arrival of a storm.

David thought it fitting, for a storm there would be. Today was their day of freedom, or he'd die trying. They would free their loved ones and kill their oppressors. There was no other way, and, to a man, felt the same. Most of the people going to the farm today were men. When they came back, they would take out the guards. Even Richard and Bill seemed subdued. He figured each man was trying to imagine what was to come.

David's body jerked as the bus pulled away. The ride seemed to take a long time. The diesel wafting up reeked; was the old bus trying to gas them? His thoughts kept wandering back to Mary. He tried not to sink into depression. It had been a long two weeks, a living hell of not knowing. The houses they passed were deserted. Some had their doors open like silent screams, while others had been nearly burned to the ground.

He hoped he could find a house that he could make a home. He hoped he could take care of Mary and, hopefully, her baby too. By the end of today, perhaps tomorrow, he would be a free man, and

Mary wouldn't have to worry about hiding. They could all breathe fresh air instead of the hateful dust of the coal mine.

The bus slowed, and he could see the farm ahead. They passed several small homes, all abandoned, all melancholy without their people. David snorted at his own melancholy thoughts, and knew it was worry for Mary that pulled him so low. He'd soon see her and know of her condition.

Gerhard stood by the long table laden with pans of steaming water. He'd be somewhat clean in a few minutes, and hopefully would never step foot in the coal mine again. The people disembarked from the bus; Miles got off as well, and stretched. The bus driver too seemed as restless as the people around him.

David walked directly over to Gerhard and shook his hand, his eyes searching the other man's face for a clue.

"How is Mary? Did she lose the baby?" he blurted, unable to control his emotions.

A slow smile spread across Gerhard's thin face, his blue eyes lighting from within. "She delivered a very healthy boy, though small, two days ago. They are both doin' good."

David's knees almost buckled, and his eyes shimmered with tears. Then they spilled over leaving tracks down his face. He dropped his head into his hands and wept, his body shaking. He could feel hands patting his back and tried to bring himself under control. He couldn't seem to stop. The dam had burst, leaving him weak. A cloth was shoved into his hand and he wiped at his face, feeling the grit scrape across it.

He finally looked up and saw his friends around him, their faces a mixture of worry and understanding. That made him want to break down once more, but he took a deep breath, letting it out slowly.

"Why don't you get cleaned up, then go see her. I know she'll want to see ya," Gerhard said, smiling kindly.

David made his way to the long table and picked up a bar of soap and began to wash the grime off his face and arms. He felt like a surgeon scrubbing for an important operation. He was going to see little Howard and wanted to be as clean as possible. Grime gone, he changed into clean coveralls.

Going into the house, he found Jutta preparing breakfast for the prisoners. He smiled, and felt his mouth tremble and his eyes began to sting with tears. She came around the table, her hands covered in flour, and pulled him into an embrace and whispered soft things. He knew he was falling apart because of all the stress. He could feel her trembling and heard her weeping. He pulled back and looked down at her face.

"Go see her. She's been waiting for you," Jutta said softly, and used her wrist to wipe at her eyes. Bits of flour fell to her breasts and she wiped at it, making it worse.

David nodded, smiling. He couldn't speak, the knot in his throat nearly choking him. He turned and made his way up the stairs, to the room where he'd left her. Standing in the doorway, he watched Mary on the bed, cradling her son. He must have made a noise, because she looked up. A beautiful, sweet smile spread across her face. David walked to the bed and sat in the chair beside it.

"David, I'm so glad you're here. Would you like to meet Howard David Deets?" she asked softly.

"Yes, please," was all he could say, and she handed over the small bundle to him. When he took it, the baby seemed so light and so small. In the swaddling, he saw a tiny face, the eyes open and looking up at him. He could feel his lips spreading in a smile.

"My God, he is beautiful, Mary. He is so tiny, but he's perfect," David said, a fingertip gently tracing the outline of the newborn's face. He looked up at her and saw tears in her eyes. He got up, sat carefully on the edge of the bed, and pulled Mary into his arms, still cradling the baby.

They both cried, and he rocked her gently. The baby began to fuss, and he laughed a little, pulling back. Mary smiled up at him, wiping her eyes.

"Thanks, I needed that. I'm so glad you're here."

David got up and sat back in the chair, the baby still in his arms. He patted Howard's small back gently, rocking a little.

"Today we will make it right, Mary. We'll end this, so you and Howard can live free and in the sunshine. So, you never have to worry again," David said solemnly.

"Just please be careful. We want you back safe. When will you all leave?"

"I'm not sure. I'll have to talk to Gerhard. It will more than likely be this afternoon, on our way back. At least Bill and Richard are with us. Miles is too. There are only two guards at the mine. I think we can take them easily," David said.

"Jutta said they found a lot of supplies. They'll be giving some out to the ones coming out of the coal mine. To get them set up. She and Gerhard are also going to be donating food and supplies."

"That's really good. It will help the families taking them in. I'm hoping to find a house with a good size yard, so I can plant a garden next year. I also plan to help Gerhard with this farm, so that others can have something as well," David said.

"Jutta found me a house just up the road. The family was down in Florida when everything stopped. Once I'm feeling up to it, I'll be moving in," Mary said, then she looked at her lap, her hands clasping and unclasping. She looked up at David, her face serious and nervous at the same time.

"Please don't think me forward, or presumptuous. I care about you, David. I know you care about me. I know it is too soon. We each have a lot of healing and grieving to be done. Jutta said the house has four bedrooms. I would like to ask you to come and stay there, live there. But no commitments, no expectations. I want to get to know you without the fear and oppression that we've been under," she said hesitantly.

David's heart somersaulted at her words, and his heart thundered in his chest. He nodded his head, trying to choose his words carefully.

"I understand. I would never step over the line, Mary. I know you are still grieving for Howard. I won't shame either of us. I want to get to know you as well. I think it is a good idea. I can care for both of you and protect you. And if and when the time comes, I'll court you as is proper."

Mary smiled up at him, her face shining and luminescent with joy. He smiled at her and then looked back down to the child.

"I promise, little man, to take care of you and your mother. I promise to honor your father, Howard Deets."

XXX

Though the clouds hung low, they threatened and argued all day, but didn't drop their aqueous load. Their slate gray forms collided and moved across the sky. Harry and Clay stood on the porch, looking out across the valley. It was cool and the air was damp. They were all feeling antsy and on edge. They would be leaving in an hour. Each of them had checked and cleaned their weapons, and gathered the extra weapons that had been confiscated, which would be passed out to the people from the mine.

Willene had insisted everyone eat a hearty meal before they left the house. Katie was in the kitchen, helping Marilyn make up dinner parcels. No one knew how long they would be gone for.

"We won't be back until they're all dead," Harry had told them.

"I'm hoping that, by this time tomorrow, it will be over, and we can start living our lives freely," Clay said.

"Me too," Harry agreed. "It has gone on way too long. It should never have happened in the first place."

The dogs were on the porch, asleep. Monroe was in the kitchen playing; it was too damp and cold to be outside, and Marilyn seemed to want him close by.

"I think I'll be able to breathe once we free the people from the coal mine. It will be the first step. Once that is done, I'm hoping the rest will go like clockwork. I'm also hoping this weather works in our favor," Harry speculated.

"It should, and if it rains, then if Boggy needs to blow up the Bluemont, it won't be too bad fire-wise, at least."

"That's what I was thinking. What worries me is, what about the women and children of these people? I'll tell you now, I won't kill a woman unless she's shooting at us," Harry said.

"Same here. I guess play it by ear. I don't know who is married and who has kids. I guess we'll have to wait and see. But the men, they are already dead; they just don't know it," Clay said.

The screen door opened, and Boggy and Earl came out. Both had coffee, and handed a cup to Harry and Clay each.

"I feel as nervous as a long-tail cat in a room full of rockin' chairs," Earl said.

"Me too," Boggy chimed in.

"I expect that's normal. We are getting ready to go to war," Harry said mildly.

"When do we leave?" Earl asked.

197

"I guess we can load up the truck now, wrap all the extra weapons and ammunition in a tarp so we can hand them out at the mine. Wilber will meet us there. We'll park about a mile out and walk in."

"Sounds like a plan," Earl said and turned, taking Boggy.

Harry figured they might as well head out. He and Clay went back into the house. Willene was coming down the stairs; she'd just put Angela down for a nap. He saw her face. There was strain there, as well as fear and a smidgen of hope.

"Well, brother, is it about time?" she asked.

"Yeah. We'll get loaded up and head out. I don't think you'll be bothered. It's been a long time since anyone has come this way. Joshua knows we're going today, so if you need him, he will be there, and his people."

"Good to know. What guns do we have here?" Willene asked.

"We're taking ours, Boggy is taking your Ruger and the AR15. He'll need the extra firepower for the bed and breakfast. I've pulled up Peapot's rifles, and there is a .38 special and a Sig Sauer that I figure you'll want to have on you," he said, pulling the gun from his waist. "I cleaned it and it's ready to go. I have a long gun up in my room, ready if you need it. There is a lock on it, and the key is on my dresser. Just didn't want Monroe getting to it," he said.

198

"Good. I doubt we'll need it, and we have the shotgun here as well," she said. They walked into the kitchen, and Katie and Marilyn stopped. Both looked frightened.

"We're going to get ready to leave," Harry said. "Alan, stay here in case something happens. I'll be counting on you to keep everyone safe." Alan had been sitting at the table eating wedding cake. His face had crumbs on it, and Harry tried not to laugh when the young man nodded in a dignified manner.

Boggy, Wilber, Earl, and Clay came into the kitchen. Clay went to Katie, took her into his arms, and held her for a few moments. The women began to tear up, though they held off crying. Harry was glad. He was already keyed up. It was a highly-charged emotional moment. They needed to keep frosty and focused on the task ahead. Harry went to Willene and hugged his twin.

"Keep them safe and I'll get back home. When, I'm not sure." Then he went to Marilyn and hugged her. She clung to him and wept softly, then kissed him on the lips. He pulled back and looked down into her eyes, then dipped his head and kissed her. He crushed her hard to him, then let her go. He went to Monroe, kissed the child's head and squeezed the back of his neck, eliciting a giggle from the boy.

199

Each of the men went to the women, hugging and kissing them goodbye in turn. Earl picked up Monroe and hugged him tight, rocking him from side to side. He kissed his head and set him back into his chair. Though Monroe sensed something was going on, he didn't seem upset by all the tears. They picked up the packages the women had packed and they all went out to the truck.

Driving down the hill with Wilber, Harry drove to Wilber's truck. He unloaded Wilber, so the old man didn't have to walk down the hill. Wilber took Clay and Earl. Boggy rode on with him. They began their drive to the coal mine. The first drops of rain began to hit the windshield. They each had rain gear, except for Wilber. Wilber said he'd get his once the men at the coal mine were dealt with.

When they were roughly a mile from the mine, they pulled up and parked their trucks out of sight of the road. From there, they carefully made their way to the mine. There were no signs of people, and the road remained empty. As they drew closer, they split up. It was quiet, and the rain, though light, covered the sound of their steps. Boggy led the way, since he knew the buildings' locations. Earl had been assigned to lead the other group.

As they moved around the abandoned buildings, Harry kept his ears attuned to all noises. He and Boggy squatted behind a stack of timber. He could see the guards. Both men were sitting inside a truck, smoke coming from the opened windows. The windshield was fogged over, and Harry figured the men wouldn't be able to see them clearly. Harry set up his rifle. He looked across the large yard and saw Wilber in place. He had also set up his weapon.

Harry dialed in on his target. Though he couldn't see the man's face clearly, he didn't need to. He just needed his head in the crosshairs. He looked up, and saw that Wilber was ready. Clay was beside him, watching Boggy.

"Okay, Boggy. Count down from three," Harry whispered. Boggy held up his fingers. Clay was to watch and count down for Wilber, who would shoot at the same time as Harry. Earl was to shoot anyone who survived or came to the guard's aid. They didn't expect anyone else to be at the mine, but they didn't want to discount the possibility.

"Three, two, one," Boggy said softly.

There was an explosion of two shots, nearly simultaneous. Blood blossomed on the windshield as the glass spiderwebbed with cracks. The men waited, holding their breaths. There were no other sounds except the dying echo of the shots, no other movements, no sounds of vehicles approaching. Nothing. Wilber stood and slowly walked out, Clay and Earl following. Harry stood and pulled his Glock, ready for movement or threat. Boggy was behind, watching and guarding his six.

The men approached the truck and Wilber opened the passenger's side door cautiously. Clay had his service weapon aimed at the occupants, should any of them be a threat. Then Harry saw him lower his weapon and holster it. He and Boggy came up to the driver's side and opened the door. In the cab were two faceless men, their faces blasted away by the high velocity shells.

Harry took the arm of the nearest man and pulled him out of the truck. Boggy helped drag him off to the side, behind large barrels. They didn't want the women from the coal mine to see them. Hiding the bodies was the best they could do. Clay did the same, and dragged the other man beside the first. He looked up at Harry and smiled grimly.

"Phase one, done. Let's get those folks out of the mine," Clay said.

They all walked over, and Clay stepped into the cage. Earl and Boggy lowered him down. After what seemed like a lifetime, the cage screeched to life and came back up. With Clay stood seven women, unbelievably thin and coated with black grit. It was all Harry could do to not go over and shoot those men again. Rage roiled through his blood, and nearly overwhelmed him. His eyes stung, but he blinked the tears back. Tamped down the anger for later, for when he needed it. He pulled off his pack and, opening it, drew out bottles of water and whatever food Willy had packed.

The cage went down again, and he began to hand out the food and water. Wilber did the same. When the next group came up, there were six, and another six came up in the last group. All were wretched, thin and in rags, and heavily coated with coal dust. Though they all wore masks, the masks themselves were heavily crusted. They were all weeping softly, and passing the food around and drinking the water. They stood huddled together, their eyes squinting in the dim light.

Harry spun when he heard a truck coming, and raised his Glock. Around him, Boggy, Earl, Wilber, and Clay did the same. A rusted-out truck pulled into the large yard. To Harry's relief, he saw that it was Boney and two old men. They all lowered their weapons.

Boney got out and walked over to Wilber and shook his hand. He surveyed the huddle of people and shook his head.

"If I could kill them bastards again, I would," he said gruffly, wiping at his eyes.

They turned as a group when they heard the chugging diesel engine of the bus. They couldn't see it yet, but could hear it.

"I brought supplies to give to them folks. Figure when they get parceled out, they'd be more welcome if they brought some food," Boney said. The two old men who'd accompanied him walked over.

"This here is the Edison twins. They're gonna be helpin' us tonight," Boney said and grinned.

Harry reached over and shook each man's hand, and Clay, Earl, and Boggy did the same. They turned and watched as the bus maneuvered into the yard, then stopped. The bus disgorged its passengers, who ran to their loved ones. Harry and his men stood back as families hugged and held on to each other. A slender man walked over to Clay. Harry saw that Clay knew him, and Clay's eyes teared up. Clay pulled the man into a bear hug.

"Jesus! Steven, you look like shit," he choked out, causing Steven to laugh and pat Clay on the back.

"Brother, you have no idea," he laughed, but a sob caught in his throat.

"This is Steven Stroh. He's a deputy," Clay said to the men around him. They each reached a hand out and shook it.

"We'll load everyone up and take them to their new homes. We've got food and supplies for them. We're going to be going after Yates and his men after it gets dark," Harry said.

A big man walked over, and Harry watched him as he shook everyone's hands.

"Not sure if you all know me. I'm David Colman. I heard what you said, and I want to come with you and help you fight."

"You're more than welcome," Harry smiled.

"Mary Deets had her baby, little Howard. They're both doing good. The baby is small, but healthy," David told Clay.

Clay shook his head. "Thanks, David. I'm relieved to hear that. I heard what Yates did to Howard. That coward. He's my target for tonight. You want to come along with me?"

"Hell yes, I do. He robbed Mary of a husband and a father to their son. That bastard has a lot to pay for," David almost snarled. Harry thought that he'd hate to be on the wrong side of this big man.

It took a bit of time to get the food and supplies passed out, and the people loaded onto the bus. Miles Whitmen, the driver, was given instructions.

"Steven, here's a Glock I took off some asshole. Use if you need it. I figure you'll need to guard these folks as they get to their destinations. Rest well, brother. We'll make it right," Clay said, handing over the weapon along with a magazine.

"Thanks. Are there any more weapons?" Steven asked.

"Yeah. We're giving one rifle to David, and one to Gideon. We've also passed out several .38 specials among your group. That should help defending the homes people end up in," Clay said.

"Good. Good luck and good hunting, Clay, and put a bullet between Yates's sorry eyes," Steven said, his eyes sheening. He coughed, holding a shaking hand to his mouth, as Harry watched. It tore at him; these people had suffered greatly.

His small group stood back as the bus pulled away. The two guards, Bill Hawkins and Richard Bibs, remained behind to help locate and kill the remaining KKK members. The men gathered at the trucks and went over their plans. It was growing late, and the night was beginning to blot out the daylight. The rain had eased up to a drizzle.

"Clay, David, and Earl, you guys can take that truck, if you don't mind the blood all over it," Harry suggested.

Clay laughed. "We can use the tarp from Boney's truck to line the seats. We just need to get the blood and gore off the windshield so I can see to drive."

"Good enough. While you hunt down your target, me, Boggy, and Wilber will head out to the Bluemont and set up there. We can sit tight there. I figure no one is going to want to be out in this rain. Once you're done, come over to us. We'll wait as long as we can. We'll also try to get a fix on a number," Harry said, then turned to Boney, and his brow raised in question.

"Me and the twins will go and hit a few houses we know are in Yates's circle of cohorts. We should be able to take 'em out," Boney grinned, and the Edison twins giggled and nudged each other.

Harry almost busted out laughing at the sight of their unconcealed glee. He hoped he was as lively as them in his senior years. Though elderly, they'd all proven themselves quite capable and competent at killing their enemy, as well as outsmarting them. Bill and Richard would accompany Harry.

XXX

Clay drove the truck while the other two men kept watch. Earl was sandwiched between the two large men, but he too tried to look out the cracked windshield. They'd done their best to get the bone and brains out of the truck, but it had ended up being a smeared mess.

"I'd wished we coulda cleaned that windshield better, I'll swear everything looks smeared," Earl said as his head bobbed up and down. Clay laughed, and looked over to David, who was looking down at the smaller man curiously. Clay winked at David, and then shrugged his shoulders.

"Well, we gave all the water away, but maybe, once we take care of Yates, we can clean it out a bit more. There are cleaning supplies in one of the closets at the precinct," Clay suggested.

"That's sounds like a plan. Glad it's a getting dark. I feel 'bout neked out here in the open. Though I reckon no one can see through the windshield," Earl said.

Clay drove slowly. He was trying to hold off on using the headlights. He'd been thinking about parking several blocks from the precinct. He wanted to take a look at the area. It had been a while, and he didn't want to go in cold.

"I was thinking about parking over by the bar, The Lazy J. Then we can walk in," Clay voiced his thoughts.

"That sounds good. There are plenty of buildings around for cover, and it would be stealthier to walk in, than drive," David agreed.

"I can't wait to put a bullet in that bastard. Poor Mary, I know she must have been heartbroken," Clay said, anger lacing his voice.

"She was, Clay, but worst, I think, was being put in that hole. I think Steven may have problems. He's had a cough for a few months now. I'm hoping it was just a reaction to all the dust, but I don't know," David said.

"You're right as rain 'bout that coal dust. It's terrible, gets everywhere," Earl agreed.

"But Mary is okay now? Healthy, I mean?" Clay asked.

"She is. She was too thin by half down there. If we hadn't have gotten her out when we did, I don't think either she or the baby would have made it. As it was, the baby was born premature," David said.

"Christ, Yates has so much to pay for. And we can only kill him once," Clay growled.

"Maybe we can kill him slow," Earl suggested softly.

Both Clay and David looked at him, and Earl looked at each man, smiling. They returned his smile. David began laughing, a low rumble at first.

"Are you thinking what I'm thinking?" he asked Clay.

"If you mean putting him down in that hole, then yes, I am," Clay laughed. Earl joined both men, smacking his knees. Soon they were all laughing, the tears coursing down their faces. They shortly brought themselves under control. Clay wiped at his eyes. An intermittent giggle threatened to surface.

"You know, Earl, I didn't know you had a hateful streak in you," Clay said laughing.

"All I can think of is that bastard hurting Monroe and his momma. I can't think of enough ways ta kill him. But I think if it lasts a long time, he'll have all that time ta think 'bout it," Earl said, all humor gone from his tone.

"True, brother, very true," Clay said, and slowed the truck down. He pulled around to the back of The Lazy J. He turned off the engine and the men sat quietly, listening to their breathing. Clay opened his door and David did as well. Earl clambered out, trying not to catch his prosthetic leg on the lip of the truck.

The rain was now light and intermittent. They followed Clay, going behind buildings and through alleyways. They took a circuitous route, stopping and listening.

"Seems like a ghost town," David said softly.

"I think it is," Clay answered.

They advanced to the back of the building that housed their prey. Clay signaled the men to either side of the back door of the precinct, and then, with his weapon ready, he cautiously opened the door. Earl followed, and David brought up the rear.

Clay paused at each door he found. He pulled out a small LED flashlight and clicked it on. His hand resting on the door knob and with the flashlight, he illuminated each room. David closed each door quietly, and they went on to the next.

They cleared all the rooms on the lower level and went up a flight of stairs. They entered the main level and froze. They heard voices. Clay recognized Yates's, but not the other. He motioned Earl and David to the left and right of him.

The men proceeded quietly, keeping to the wall. David was to ensure no one came up from behind. They got to the door to Yates's office and could hear him talking to someone. Clay took a deep breath and then opened the door, his gun targeting Yates, while Earl and David came behind, their weapons zeroing in on the other person in the room.

CHAPTER TEN

Boney drove slowly. He had the addresses to their targets. First, they were going to Murphy Tweet's home, which was just on the outskirts of town. The twins were silent as they drove. His eyes were sharp as they kept watch out the window. There were no signs of life on either the road, or in the buildings and homes.

"I ain't seen a candle in the window for a while. Seems like this whole town is dead," Ralph said softly.

"It sure does, brother. Spooky too," Abram agreed.

"You sissies, hush. Keep focused on the task at hand," Boney warned. He had to admit, it was spooky. He shivered a little, though it wasn't from the damp chill that permeated the truck. What bothered Boney was that he didn't know if Tweet had a family in his home. It would be tricky. They didn't want to kill the wives, and especially not the children. He slowed the truck down and pulled off to the side. Shutting off the engine, he looked over to the twins, who were barely discernible in the dark.

"We'll go in, take a gander in the window. If there are kids, I'll knock on the door. I'll pretend I'm lost or something. You boys keep your guns sighted on the target, but for Christ sakes don't shoot, 'cause you'll end up hittin' me."

The brothers nodded their heads, and the men got out of the truck. They walked the three hundred feet up the road, using a shielded flashlight. None of them needed to break a hip on this mission. When they got to the yard, Ralph went one way while Abram went the other. Boney walked slowly up to the house. Several lights flickered in the windows.

Coming around to the side of the house, he found an old milk crate. The yard was littered with trash. He had to step over numerous objects and prayed he wouldn't give off his position. Going up to one of the brighter windows, he set the crate on the ground and climbed up. The sight that met him both broke his heart and made his blood boil.

Two small children were asleep on a torn-up couch, looking much like two tiny puppies. Even from his vantage, he could see they were thin. Murphy, and Boney assumed, his wife, were at the table, where a lantern sat. Both were passed out, needles lying there on the table. They were junkies, and their children had been left to witness their use and fend for themselves should they wake.

He fought the tears of anger back and stepped down from the crate. Not bothering to shield his flashlight, he made his way back to the front of the house. He waved the twins to him and waited as they made their way over.

213

"They got two young'uns in there. Pitiful. I'm gonna go in. I'll hand each of you a baby an' you take 'em to the truck."

Both men nodded, their faces surprised, but said nothing. Boney turned and went to the front door. He had his long knife out and ready. He set his long gun next to the door. Stepping into the house, he was hit with a stench that made him gag. He swallowed it down, and kept his eyes on the two adults, who, thankfully, were out cold.

He stepped over the garbage that littered the floor. Empty pill containers were scattered about. He placed his hands on the first child, then froze. His heart dropped into his stomach and the hairs raised on his body. The child was dead. His hands went to the other child, and the tears fell. The other was dead as well. He backed up from them and brought his shaking hand to his mouth, trying to silence the sobs.

His head swiveled over to the man. He'd started moving, making signs of waking up. Boney stepped quickly over to the man, grabbed his mop of filthy hair, and pulled the man's head back. Murphy's eyes fluttered open, bloodshot. They opened wider when they focused on Boney's angry face.

Boney took his long knife and drew it across the man's neck with such strength and force from the grief and rage, that he nearly decapitated the

214

man. Warm blood splashed across the table and onto Boney's hand. The woman began to stir as the warm blood bathed her. Boney let go of Murphy's head and shoved the body over. He stepped over to the woman, whose eyes opened, then opened even wider when she caught sight of the bloody stranger.

He grabbed her by her hair and drew his knife across the side of her neck. She fell to the floor, clutching her neck, desperately trying to stem the flow of blood that was gushing out. Her eyes were uncomprehending, still high from whatever she'd injected into her veins. Boney felt a presence behind him and whirled around to see the twins crying. They were over by the two children curled up on the couch.

"What kind of monsters are these people?" Ralph said, his voice breaking.

"The worst kind. Let's burn this place to the ground," Boney said in a dead voice. He saw the nods of his friends and reached for the lantern. He stepped back, then threw it at Murphy's body. The glass shattered and lamp oil splashed over the body and the table. The fire rushed after it. Boney stepped back, then went to the couch and laid a raggedy blanket over the children. It was the best funeral he could give them. He'd avenged their deaths on their careless and selfish parents.

The three men exited the house as the fire spread quickly. There was a lot of trash for it to burn. Boney could hear the other men openly weeping as they stood in the yard, backing up slowly as the fire inside grew. Within ten minutes, the whole house was engulfed in flames.

"Those poor little babies. I know they're with Jesus, but it sure does break my heart," Abram said.

"Mine too, brother," Ralph said, and put an arm around his twin's shoulders. The men walked away from the burning house.

It was a dark thing, Boney thought.

They made their way back to the truck and sat in silence for a few minutes, gathering themselves. Boney pulled out a handkerchief and blew his nose and wiped his eyes. He wanted the anger and rage to subsume the grief of it all and eradicate it. He needed that rage, because the grief was killing him.

He started the truck and made a U-turn in the road and headed for Reece Archer's house. He sure as hell hoped they didn't have any children. Reece was in his early fifties, so the kids, if he had any, may not be living with him. He hoped so. They drove in silence, no one wanting to speak. From time to time, one of the twins would shudder out a sigh.

It took twenty minutes, but eventually they pulled off to the side of the road. He looked at the twins. "If you boys wanna sit this one out, I'll understand," Boney said kindly.

"Naw. We'll got to watch your six. I don't mind kill'en," Ralph said for both of them.

Nodding, Boney got out of the truck. The twins followed and came around the vehicle. They were at a trailer park, and it looked like a graveyard to Boney. No signs of life. The men walked between trailers, working their way toward the one that had a light flickering like a beacon. Boney nodded for the men to spread out; he could see someone moving around. He set up his rifle, stuffing an old hat beneath to balance it on the roof of a car.

They had brought a glass bottle of lamp oil with a rag sticking out. Abram was to throw the Molotov cocktail at the trailer door. Abram had the best arm, since he'd played a lot of ball in his youth. Boney watched as he got closer to the trailer. He saw a flicker of light when Abram lit it, then saw the man haul his arm back and throw the bottle of flame. It arced beautifully and hit the door square, spreading lamp oil all over the door.

The people inside began to scramble around. The door shot open and Reece came out, a semi-automatic weapon spewing ammo. Abram had got down low behind a car and stayed out of sight. Boney took a breath and lined up the shot calmly. He pulled the trigger, and Reece dropped to the ground. Another man came out, and Boney chambered another round. He took aim and dropped the man.

Someone inside broke out a window and began shooting. It was now dark inside the trailer. Boney looked over at Ralph, who was lining up a shot. He figured the man was lining up on the muzzle flashes from the shots. Two more shots came, then Ralph's rifle barked, and all was quiet.

Boney stood quietly, then after a few minutes, walked toward the trailer. Abram got up from the ground unsteadily. Boney listened but could hear nothing from the trailer. He walked to Abram, who was clutching an arm. He'd been hit, but otherwise seemed okay.

"You okay, brother?" Ralph asked.

"Just a scratch," Abram grinned.

"You boys stay out here and keep an eye out for anyone. I'm going in, see what's what," Boney announced.

He clicked on his flashlight and walked over to the dead men by the door of the trailer. The fire had burned itself out, and he stepped over the corpses and up into the trailer. Cautiously he looked around the corners. There were cards on the table. He'd interrupted their game, apparently. He walked to the back of the trailer, and into the room where the shooter had been. A man's body was slumped in front of the window. Ralph had taken a good shot. He whirled around when he heard a noise, and could have kicked himself for being so careless.

In the corner of the room was a bed, and on it was a woman, crouched in the corner, her arm chained to the bed's headboard. She was naked and crying, trying to curl in on herself.

"Hush, young lady, it's all over with. They won't hurt you no more," Boney said softly as he took the blanket off the bed and wrapped it around the shivering woman.

"He's got the key in his pocket," she said, her voice trembling.

Boney nodded and kicked the dead man over and patted his pockets. He found the key and went to the chain and unlocked the padlock. He helped her up and looked around. "Do you got any clothes? Any personal stuff?"

She nodded and pointed to a closet. He went over and opened it, and found woman's clothing on the floor of the closet. He picked it up and handed it to her. He turned his back so she could get dress.

"I'm done mister. Thank you for saving me," she said, still crying. But she was gathering her control, he could see.

"I'll take you home, honey, don't you worry," he assured her.

"I ain't got a home," she said, then started crying again. "They killed my folks and they stole me. I ain't got no place to go."

"Don't you worry your head none. You'll come ta live with me. An' iffin that don't suit, we'll find

219

another place for you. You ain't alone. What's your name, honey?"

"Megan," she said, and followed him as he led the way out of the trailer.

"Megan, I'm Boney, and these here are my friends, Ralph and Abram. They're good men." Both men looked surprised, then nodded to her. Boney saw a truck parked by the trailer. He walked over and patted each of the dead man's pockets. Finding nothing, he went back into the trailer and came back out with a set of keys.

"Ralph, you think you can drive?" Boney asked.

"Sure, I can. Come on, Abram, I'll take ya ta see Doc. We'll let them know the progress," Ralph promised Boney.

"Okay. Tell the women we'll bring back their men, and tell Alan I'll bring back his grandpa," Boney said.

He turned to Megan. "They're going to a safe place. Did you want to go with them?"

"No. I want ta stay with you, Boney. Is that okay?" she asked.

"It sure is. My truck is down here a piece. We're gonna head to another place to rout out some peckerwoods. Just like we done here." He grinned at her.

The truck with Abram and Ralph passed them and tooted the horn. Boney snorted. So far, only one injury. That was good. He would head over to the Bluemont and see what he could do to help.

XXX

Yates looked up in surprise, and then the color faded from his face. Clay had his weapon aimed at his head. He moved in and then to the side, letting David in, whose weapon was trained on the other man.

"On the floor, Yates. You know the drill better than anybody," Clay commanded.

"Don't think about it, asshole," he heard David say.

Yates raised his head and came around his desk, arms raised. He got down on his knees, then down on his stomach. He put his hands up on the back of his neck and laced his fingers together.

"Earl, pat him down, check his ankle, make sure no weapons," Clay ordered.

Earl came around, the AR15 pointed at Yates's head. He carefully maneuvered, keeping behind the man. The barrel of the weapon pressed to Yates's head. Clay's eyes never left Yates. When Earl was finished, he pulled out the cuffs Clay had given him. Clay had showed Earl over and over how to cuff a man until Earl could do it in a smooth motion. He did Clay proud, cuffing Yates expertly. He stood back.

"Go to his desk and get another set of cuffs," Clay said, then looked over to the man David was guarding. Clay didn't know him, didn't care. David shoved the man to the floor, and when the man started to rise, David placed his foot in the middle of his back and put a considerable amount of his weight down, causing the man to cry out and put his hands on his head.

Earl came over and patted the man down as well. He pulled out a knife from the man's boot. Also, a small .22 from the man's waistband. Earl stuck that in his back pocket. He then cuffed the man from behind.

"So, what are you going to do, Clay? Shoot us while we're cuffed?" Yates sneered.

Clay started laughing, which caused Earl and David to start laughing. The men laughed so hard that Clay had to sit down. David followed suit, and found a chair to sit in. Earl sat on the side of Yates's desk. It took a bit of time to get the laughter under control. Clay knew it was nerves and relief. But it was with the knowledge that these men wouldn't die quickly.

"Earl, go get the truck. Then we'll load them up," Clay said, wiping the tears away from his face, a giggle escaping now and then. He looked at Yates, who was bright red.

He leaned forward, his elbows on his knees. His hands hung loose between them, though he did have a good grip on his weapon.

"No, Danny, we aren't going to shoot you. We are, however, going to give you a dose of your own medicine."

David started humming, and Clay looked over, grinning. It was hard not to laugh; it felt so damn good. These men had tried to kill him and Katie. They deserved nothing less than a prolonged death.

"What the hell is that supposed to mean, you monkey's ass," the other man snarled.

David stood, walked over and kicked the man in the ribs. There was an audible crunch and the man cried out in pain, rolling. He couldn't do much with his arms cuffed behind him.

"Shut up, or I'll make it worse," David said softly, and put his large boot up by the man's mouth.

Clay smiled. He knew David was a good guy, but he got the sense David was in love with Mary. When he'd talked about her, his face had fairly glowed. That was between him and Mary. If she cared about David, that was all that mattered. He knew Howard had loved his wife enough to want her to be safe and happy.

Earl came back in, a huge smile on his face. He'd brought rope with him.

"Figured we'd tie up their feet. Don't want them runnin' away afore we get to the fun part," he sniggered, his face flushed bright red.

He went over to each man and looped the rope so it would hinder their strides. Then David and Clay picked each man up, taking them by the arm and leading them at a slow shuffle out the door. Earl ran ahead to the truck and put down the tailgate. Clay and David picked the men up in turn and slung them into the bed of the tuck, eliciting a scream from the injured man.

"I'll sit back here with them, make sure they don't try anything funny," David volunteered.

"Sounds good. Come on, Earl, get in the truck," Clay said.

"Don't gotta tell me twice," he said and chuckled.

Clay pulled away from the building and accelerated fast. He wanted to get these men to the coal mine quickly. Harry and Boggy might need them. He pulled out onto the main drag and sped up. His heart was racing, and he felt exhilaration at the knowledge that he and Katie could live as husband and wife, free from this bastard's tyranny.

The loss of power had been brutal on everyone, there was no doubt, but Yates and his ilk had compounded the problems, causing fear and mistrust and death. They had exacerbated an already horrendous situation.

He and Audrey had destroyed the town with their notion of paradise. Surely anything built on hate could not stand for long. He and the remaining people would make sure that Yates and his kind never took hold of their town again.

Earl was quiet in the truck. He kept looking around.

"You okay, Earl?" he asked.

"Yeah. I'm just watching to make sure no one stops us, Clay. We need ta make sure this animal is put down for good."

"You see anyone in our way that wants to stop us, just wave hello to them with your AR15," Clay grinned.

Earl sniggered, and smacked Clay on the shoulder. Clay slowed down for a turn, then sped up once more. He kept checking his mirror but saw no movements from David. Then he made the final turn that led to the mine. Clay pulled up to the opening and pointed the headlights to the cage. He and Earl got out, and David jumped down from the back of the truck.

Clay walked over and opened the tailgate and they pulled the men out by their ankles. They were still hobbled. David took the injured man and led him to the cage. Clay and Earl grabbed a now-struggling Yates and dragged him to the cage as well.

225

"What the hell, Clay? What are you playing at?" Yates shouted. Clay didn't answer until he'd shoved Yates in beside the other man and closed the cage. Earl went to the controls, David standing with him.

"I'm sending you into hell, Danny, the same place where you sent women and children. You'll spend the rest of your short life down there, in the dark and alone. Well, almost alone."

"What? What the hell. Take these cuffs off! You can take us out of town and drop us off. We won't come back," the man cried, looking from Yates to Clay.

Clay nodded, and David and Earl started lowing the cage.

"No, you'll both die of either thirst or starvation. Or maybe, if you're lucky, you'll fall down into a deep hole. You know, instant death," Clay said.

"Then kill us now, Clay, kill us now," Sheriff Yates pleaded, his voice high with panic.

David laughed. "Sheriff, I hope your death is a long and painful one. You hurt so many people. You killed loved ones without regard or care for your actions. Die slowly, Danny, die slowly."

"Bye, asshole," Earl called, and laughed as the cage lowered out of sight.

Both the injured man and Yates screamed from below, their voices fading. Their voices growing fainter, until the screech of the gears overpowered them. Then the gears stopped. Clay and the other two men stood near the opening, but they could hear nothing. If the men were screaming, it didn't reach them.

"Oh dang, how is they gonna get out of that cage? Their hands are cuffed behind them," Earl laughed suddenly.

"I guess they aren't," David grunted.

Clay spat down into the hole. He looked at David and smiled. "Rest in peace, Howard. We've avenged your murder."

"Amen," David and Earl said together.

XXX

Harry had parked his truck a quarter mile from the bed and breakfast. Boggy and Wilber got out of the truck cab, while Bill and Richard climbed out of the back. Harry looked around, but there was no movement on the street. He could see candles flickering in windows, but only from a few houses. The rest were dark and quiet.

Boggy walked around the truck, carrying a bag of dynamite sticks and blasting caps. The other men gathered around. Harry looked at them. He knew Wilber and Boggy could handle themselves, but he didn't know about Bill and Richard.

"Bill, since I don't know you or Richard, you'll be our backup. You'll watch our six," Harry said.

"Watch your what?" Bill asked.

"It means you watch our asses," Wilber snorted in disgust.

"Oh, sorry," Bill said.

"Clay and his group should join us, so don't shoot them. Also, don't forget about Boney. Stay down, stay quiet," Harry ordered.

Both of the new men nodded, their faces illuminated with fear. Harry knew they were afraid, they were all afraid, but they were more afraid of living in this hell. It had to end, and it had to end now.

In the distance, they saw headlights, and the group froze. Everyone disappeared into the trees or behind abandoned vehicles. Harry pulled his Glock. He saw Boggy take out his Ruger. Silently, everyone waited. The truck slowed down and drew closer. Then Harry stepped from the trees and holstered his weapon.

Boggy followed, then Wilber. The truck pulled up beside the group. Boney leaned out and grinned.

"Made it here ta babysit you kids," Boney laughed.

"You old bastard! Glad you could make it to the party," Wilber said and sniggered. Then he leaned in, and everyone else looked into the truck as well. Harry saw a young woman wrapped in a quilt.

"Megan? Is that you?" Wilber asked in confusion.

"Yeah, Pop Pop, it's me," Megan said.

"You know this girl?" Boney asked Wilber.

"Yeah. She's a classmate of Alan's. Or she was. What happened, honey?" Wilber asked.

"Some men killed Mommy and Dad. Then they took me and kept me locked up. They hurt me, Pop Pop," Megan said, and started crying again. Wilber pulled the girl out of the truck, held her in his arms, and rocked her. The men stood around, their eyes fill with sorrow and tears.

"Oh, honey, we didn't know. I'm so sorry, we didn't know," was all Wilber could say. Harry looked over to Bill and Richard. Their faces were a rictus in sorrow and shame. He wondered if they'd known.

He walked over to them. "Did you boys know about this?" Harry asked them, his voice rough.

Both men shook their heads, and Bill wiped his eyes. "No, we didn't," Bill explained. "We didn't know. Because we wasn't as enthusiastic as they wanted us ta be, we were kind of like outcasts. We was good enough to work, but not good enough for the inner circle."

"If we had known it, we'd have done something," Richard said, wiping the tears off his face. "I know you think we're dirt, and that's okay, 'cause we went along with things. But we never thought things would go so bad and so wrong. We didn't know so many people would be hurt."

Harry looked at both men. He didn't think they were bad, just weak. They'd chosen the wrong side but had been brought over. He nodded to them.

"Megan, you'll need to stay in the truck," Harry told the girl, who'd managed to get herself under control again.

"Bill and Richard will guard you and keep you safe. Please keep quiet and stay put. It is going to get loud and dangerous soon."

"Yes sir," she said, and Wilber helped her get back into the truck.

"You stay here, honey, and when this is finished, I'll take you ta see Alan," Wilber said and patted her hand.

"Thanks, Pop Pop."

Harry turned to the men, and they to him.

"This should be the last of them. At least, I hope. With Yates gone, and most of the ringleaders gone, it should break their backs. Shoot anyone that comes out of that house that has a weapon. If they are men, kill them, with or without a weapon. No one lives. We kill it here and we kill it now," Harry said darkly.

"You damn right," Boney said.

They turned and walked up the road, their steps cautious, their eyes searching. Boggy brought up the rear with Wilber, while Harry and Boney took the lead. They looked around, into darkened homes.

Night frogs began, it sounded sweet and peaceful after the rain having let up, chirruped into the night.

They heard distant laughter, and paused.

Harry signaled for them to go forward. Then Boggy hissed, and everyone stopped. Harry turned to look back at Boggy and saw lights. The men bled into the trees and behind bushes. Harry watched as a vehicle came to a stop near the trucks, and a big man got out. He let out a breath. It was Clay.

Bringing out his flashlight, he blinked it on and off. He waited, and the signal was returned. Clay, David, and Earl quickly approached. Boney and Wilber were whispering to each other, but he couldn't hear what they were saying. It only took a minute before the three men reached them.

"How did it go, Clay?" Harry asked softly.

"Put Yates and some other shit heel in the coal mine. Sent them down in the cage, tied up. Figure they'll die a slow death, which is what they deserve."

Harry let out a low chuckle. "Damn, you're good."

Clay laughed. "It was Earl's idea, really."

Harry looked at Earl, his eyebrows raised. Earl grinned shyly and shrugged.

"I think we all kinda thought that one up. We didn't want that jackass to die too fast. A bullet was too good for him."

"You said it, brother," Boggy said.

Earl smacked Boggy on the back good-
naturedly. Harry smacked Earl on the back and
laughed, shaking his head. He had to hand it to
them, that was a good ending for the sheriff.

Everyone checked their weapons. They walked
slowly toward the three-story house. It had seen
better days. Apparently, Jeff Bluemont had not
taken care of his grandmother's house. They could
hear laughter more clearly now.

"It sounds like a lot of them fellers is in there. I
think, maybe, Boggy set one of the sticks and we let
it blow. That should get the ants a-swormin' out of
the anthill," Boney suggested.

"Yeah. We can position ourselves and pick
them off," Harry said.

"I think it's a sound plan," David agreed.
"There are seven of us. We're all good shots, and if
they try to get dug in, I have a fair arm at tossing
another stick if you have it."

Harry grinned. "Yes, we have another stick.
We'll hold that in reserve and, as you say, if they
dig in, we'll blow them out."

The men scattered, some farther out from the
house. Harry positioned himself behind the engine
block of a dead car. Boggy squatted beside him and
took out a stick and a blasting cap. Harry handed
him a lighter. Boggy crept toward the house,
keeping low. Harry had his sights aimed just
beyond him. He watched as Boggy crept low, then

went to the house. Beneath the house was an open crawl space that had once been covered with lattice work. Most of it was torn away now.

Harry saw the flame from Boggy's lighter flicker, then darkness. Then he spotted Boggy hauling ass at a low crouch, and Harry covered his retreat. Boggy arrived back to the vehicle and picked up his rifle. He brought it up and aimed it at the house, waiting.

They could see figures moved within the house, and laughter floated out through the cracks. Harry was about to ask Boggy how long before the thing would blow up when there was a tremendous explosion. Harry could feel the ground and the car vibrate, and the shockwave passed over. He didn't know what he'd expected, but this was impressive. He yawned to clear his ears and focused on the house. The front half of the house had been blown off. From beyond, they could hear men calling. Some were screaming.

Harry lifted his weapon and sighted a man stumbling out. Before he could take a shot, someone, Boney, he thought, shot the man in the chest. He collapsed where he stood. There was a lot of shouting now, and confusion. Another man ventured down the stairs, and another shot went off.

This time it was Boggy. The man tumbled down the rest of the stairs. Harry saw movement in the third story window. This time he took aim and

233

shot. The man fell through the bottom half of the window and got stuck, his upper torso hanging out. The gun in his hand fell to the ground.

There was a shot from inside, but no one returned it. *Good*, he thought. *They're waiting until they have a target.*

He could hear Boggy breathing, though it wasn't fast. He looked over, and Boggy looked at him and grinned. He smiled and smacked Boggy on the back. Everyone waited patiently. Someone stuck their head up and got hit; by whom, he didn't know. It could have been Earl or Wilber.

It was now a waiting game. Four down, unknown how many to go. He could hear Clay and David talking in low voices. There was another volley of shots from inside the house. No one returned fire.

"Okay, we give up. We're coming out. Our hands are up. Don't shoot," someone called.

There was no response. Four men came out, hands raised. One was limping badly. They tried to descend the torn-up steps in the dark. Harry saw Boggy aim his rifle. He did the same. They fired. Two men went down, and the other two tried to scramble back into the house. Two more shots rang out, and those two dropped.

Silence fell, there were no other sounds. Harry sat down on the ground behind the truck. He reloaded his weapon.

"You think there is any more in there?" Boggy asked softly.

"I don't know. I figure we can sit for a bit and relax. I'm sure that if there is anyone else in there, they'll make some noise in a while. I'm in no hurry," Harry said.

He heard Boggy's soft laughter, and the boy sat down beside him. Both men looked up into the sky. The clouds were scuttling away, and Harry could now see starlight. There were several fires from the house that illuminated the immediate vicinity, but it was dark where they sat.

There came a rustle, and Harry and Boggy got back up. Looking through his sights, Harry scanned the area. He didn't see any movements. Then he saw Boney working over toward him.

"What do ya think? Should we send another stick over?" Boney asked.

"I was thinking maybe just set it afire. It is about trashed now. I have a couple bottles filled with lamp oil. We can light those and toss them into the house. What do you think?" Harry asked.

"I think it's time for a barbecue," Boney sniggered.

"I'll go get the bottles," Boggy said, and headed back to the trucks.

Everyone waited in silence. Time seemed to slow down. Earl made his way over, looking like a crab as he tried to keep his body low and his legs working together. They saw the silhouette of Boggy coming back with two bottles. When he got back, he squatted behind the vehicle. Two large shapes moved to them, Clay and David. They hunkered down.

"What's the plan, Harry?" Clay asked.

"I don't think we need to use more dynamite. A couple of these will burn the rest out if there are any hold-outs," Harry said, indicating the bottles.

"Let me throw one of those bad boys. I've always wanted to do that," David said and leered.

"You Army pukes are into that kind of shit?" Clay laughed.

"And you squids are just jealous we have all the fun," David laughed. Boggy sniggered at them both, and Harry laughed and shook his head.

"Well, one of you girls get over there and throw 'em, fir Christ sakes," Boney said.

Boggy pulled out the lighter and flicked a flame to life. David took one bottle, and Clay the other. They dipped the rags that protruded from the bottle and let them hang over the flame in turn. They caught immediately, and both men ran toward the house. They each launched their package, then ran back to the safety of the vehicle. The bottles landed true, and fire crawled along the surface covered in lamp oil.

Harry looked around. All the men were clustered around the small car. They watched as the flames licked the house and began going up its sides. The interior lit up like a Roman candle. They could now smell the smoke as it began to reach them, along with the sickly-sweet stench of burning flesh and echoes of the loud crackling and popping of wood. Then sporadic shots came, and the men tensed for another fight.

"Don't fret. Just the ammo them peckerheads had on 'em. I reckon there'll be a lot of that for a bit," Boney announced.

The fire grew exponentially, and a brilliant glow surrounded the conflagration. All of the men walked forward toward the house. If there had been anyone alive in there, they were no more. The entire house was engulfed, and the heat reached out to them.

The men stood quietly watching, and for Harry it was a significant sight. They had burned the old regime out. They had destroyed their hateful enemy.

His shoulders sagged in relief. It was done. There had been no serious injuries to his friends, whom he'd come to care for deeply. They could all look toward a future now. A difficult one, to be sure, but a future still.

"Well, folks, this is fun an' all, but I'm plum tuckered out. I think I'll head home," Boney said.

The other men grunted, and they all walked back to the trucks, the massive bonfire behind them illuminating their way.

"You boys can take that truck," Harry said, indicating the bloodied one. He was talking to Bill and Richard.

"I'll catch a ride with you guys, if you don't mind dropping me off at Gerhard's farm," David added.

"Yeah, we can do that. Thanks for the truck," Bill said. He turned to the men and shook each of their hands.

"Thank you for what you did. I'm just sorry it happened at all," Richard said.

Harry watched as the men loaded up into the truck. They pulled out and drove away. Boney went to his truck and looked in. Megan was bundled up.

"Did you want to go with me, or did you want to go with Wilber? I think Alan would love to see ya," Boney said, a gentle smile on his face.

"I think I'll go with Pop Pop," she said. "Thank you for saving me."

Boney helped her out of his truck, and she gave him a hard hug. He patted her covered shoulders and kissed the top of her head.

Getting in, he leaned out his window. "It has been an honor and a pleasure, gentlemen. Come by in a couple days, Harry. I think I found you an old-fashioned buckboard wagon. Also got a bead on a couple of horses. Make sure you bring some good stuff ta trade fir it," he said, a broad smile on his weathered face.

Harry laughed, and patted the top of the truck.

"Thanks, Boney. After all the dust settles, me and Earl will stop by. Thanks again for all your help."

The group watched as Boney pulled away. Wilber took Megan to his truck and helped her inside. Clay got in as well. Harry, Boggy, and Earl got into his truck and they pulled out, heading home.

XXX

Harry and Earl stood on the porch. The sun was just peeking over the mountains. The air was crisp and damp and clean.

"My God, I can't believe it is over," Earl said softly. He held a steaming coffee cup in both hands.

"Me either. My body almost feels weak with the relief of it," Harry agreed.

They heard laughter in the kitchen. Wilber would be taking Alan home today. They were taking Megan with them. Alan had been happy to see her, and they had sat up talking the rest of the night.

The screen door opened and Clay, Boggy, and Katie came out, each with a cup of coffee. The children were still asleep upstairs. Boggy had a bag over his shoulder, and a shovel in his free hand.

"What are you up to?" Harry asked Boggy.

"I'm gonna head up the road to that switchback, 'bout two miles from here, that heads to Lexington. I'm gonna blow the rocks down on that stretch of road so ain't nobody from Lexington can come our way without a lot of trouble," Boggy grinned.

"Damn fine idea. Need help?" Harry asked.

"Naw. Just need your truck is all," Boggy smiled.

Harry dug into his pocket and pulled out the truck keys. He traded Boggy's empty coffee cup for them. They watched as Boggy walked down the hill and through the barricade. Harry had left his truck below, no longer worried about hiding it.

Boggy drove away.

Marilyn, Willene, and Wilber came out onto the porch. Everyone took a seat in companionable silence. They could hear a whippoorwill in the woods, and mourning doves. The sun was now shining up and over the mountains. The leaves on the trees were beginning to color. The sky was a brilliant robin's egg blue. It would be a beautiful day.

After some time, there was an explosion, and the shock rattled the farmhouse. The explosion startled Marilyn and Willene. Behind them, the porch door opened, and Alan and Megan came out, both wrapped in quilts.

"What in the heck was that?" Alan asked.

"That was Boggy blowing the side of the mountain. Sealing us off from Lexington," Harry said mildly, he smiled down at Marilyn.

"I guess this means we're safe," Willene said quietly.

"Yeah. I think our lives will be better off now that Yates, Audrey, and their people are gone. Any others that crop up will be dealt with in the same expedient manner," Harry said, raising his cup in salute.

"Amen," Earl said.

EPILOGUE
FIVE YEARS LATER

Harry and Earl carried baskets of food down to the wagon. The sky was just turning pink, dawn moving night out of its way. Boggy followed behind with a bundle of quilts. Monroe carried two jugs of water.

Harry placed the baskets of food to the back of the wagon. Monroe handed him the jugs, and Harry lifted up the hinged padded seats and placed the water inside the storage area. Willene and Marilyn had done a wonderful job making the hard seats comfortable with the padded cushions.

They were heading to town for Freedom Day, which they celebrated every year on the anniversary of the destruction of the KKK's grip on the town. It was also a time to trade and meet up with friends. Because of the distance, they only went to town every few months.

The men walked back up the hill.

"Looks like it's gonna be a pretty day for travelin'," Earl said.

"It sure does, Uncle Earl," eleven-year-old Monroe said. Monroe was getting tall now and had taken on a lot of the heavy chores around the house.

"Go make sure your sisters are ready to go, Monroe. You know how they like to play around,"

Harry said, and the boy ran ahead of them, Charley trying to keep up. The dog was getting older, and Harry thought he might see if there were any puppies available in town.

They reached the porch, and Marilyn came out with a cup of coffee. Harry kissed her and took the cup.

"Morning, honey. How'd you sleep?" he asked his wife. Marilyn smiled at him and smoothed his hair back. He knew he needed a haircut.

"Okay. The baby was moving around a lot. Thanks for letting me sleep in," she said and smiled up at him.

Harry laughed. "Sounds like you're having a boy, just like Monroe. He's as busy a kid as I've seen."

"You may be right. Kimberly is as mellow a child as I've seen," Marilyn laughed, and turned as their three-year-old daughter came out onto the porch. She held a cloth doll clutched to her chest, her large eyes looking up at her parents.

Harry bent and picked his daughter up. He looked into her eyes, which were just like his, one brown and the other hazel. Her dark ringlets framed her sweet face. She wrapped her chubby arms around her father's neck.

"I'm sleepy," she said softly.

"You can sleep on the trip. Go lay on the couch and I'll fetch you when we get ready to leave," Harry said softly, kissing his daughter's forehead.

"Angela's sleeping there," she complained.

"That's okay. Go sleep with her," he said, and set her down. He and Marilyn watched as their daughter staggered back into the house. Marilyn laughed.

Willene came out with another basket and handed it to her brother. "This should be the last of it. I'll make sure the girls go potty before we leave. I've also packed some fried eggs and biscuits to eat on the way, and I'll be bringing a couple of thermoses of coffee."

"Sounds good," Harry said. He turned to Marilyn. "Did you want to get a couple more quilts?" he asked his wife.

"Sure, yeah. That way, we can all snuggle down," she said, and went back into the house. Harry took the basket down the hill to the waiting wagon. The horses were hobbled, so they didn't have to worry. Monroe had already fed the chickens and milked the cow. All chores had been completed. It was a four-hour ride to town, and it would be a long ride back this afternoon, but no one minded.

XXX

Alan hitched up the small buggy to the horse. His wife, Megan came out with several baskets of goods. Homer followed her, his tail wagging. It was nearly noon. The sun was warm on his shoulders and Alan turned to take the baskets from Megan.

"I can't wait to see everyone," Alan grinned.

"Me either. They'll get to meet Wilber now," Megan said of their two-month-old son.

"I wish Pop Pop could have met him," Alan said sadly.

"Me too, honey," Megan said softly, and kissed her husband on his head. Alan secured the baskets and checked the straps on the horse. His grandfather had died in his sleep two years ago. He'd been heartbroken, but he knew his grandfather was at rest.

He saw one of his neighbors walking toward town and lifted a hand in greeting.

"How goes it?" he called.

"All's good, Deputy Alan," the man grinned.

"Headin' into town?" Alan asked.

"Sure am. Me and the missus will head out in a bit. Wouldn't miss it for the world," the man laughed.

Alan grinned, and turned as Megan came out with their son. He was bundled up tight against any chills. Alan helped her up into the small buggy, and then got up beside her. He gathered the reins and snapped them smartly. The buggy jerked, and they headed into town.

XXX

David walked back from the farm. He'd helped Jutta and Gerhard with the wagons. They would swing by to pick himself and Mary up in an hour. Mary was out in the yard when he arrived, hanging laundry. He saw her and smiled.

"Everything about ready?" she asked.

"Yeah. All three wagons are loaded. Jutta is running around frantic. Milly is about to bust; I think that baby will come any day now," David laughed.

"Yeah, I saw her yesterday. She looks miserable. Jutta thinks she's having twins," Mary laughed, grimacing. Just then, Howard came busting through the front door.

"Mommy, Rachael is crying. She's hungry, Mommy." The five-year-old fretted about his baby sister.

"I'll get her," David laughed. He walked into the house, Howard trailing him.

"Why is she crying, Daddy?" Howard asked.

"Because she wants up and is excited to go to town," David laughed. He picked up his thirteen-month-old daughter and brought her to him and kissed her cheek.

"Let me, let me," Howard said, and David held the child low for Howard to kiss. He then set his daughter down and Howard grabbed her hand.

"Easy, honey. Let her walk on her own," David said softly.

"Okay, Daddy. When are we gonna leave?" Howard asked.

"Soon. We're waiting on Aunt Jutta to get everyone ready, then they'll come by with the wagons and pick us up. Let's go out and help your mom finish hanging laundry," David suggested.

"Okay, Daddy. Come on, Rachael, we gotta help Mommy," Howard said, and flew out of the house.

XXX

Katie came downstairs. Clay had just come home from the office. He was officially off today but wore his uniform. He walked over and kissed his wife.

"About ready to head to the park?" he asked.

"Yeah. The kids are as ready as they'll ever be," she laughed. They looked up as the twin boys come through from the kitchen. The four-year-old brothers had an apple each, huge in their small hands.

"You boys ready to go?" Clay asked.

"Yeah, Daddy. We ready," Mark answered, and Kyle nodded solemnly, his large dark eyes serious. Clay bent and picked both boys up in his arms, and they wrapped their sticky fingers around his neck, the apples falling to the ground.

"Uh oh," Kyle said.

"It's okay, honey. We can leave them here, and I'll wash them when we get back," Katie assured her son.

"Okay, Mommy," Mark said.

They left the house and walked down the sidewalk. They passed several families also heading to the park. Mayor Mary Lou Jaspers would be setting things up at the bandstand. She had found old bunting years ago, and each year she decorated the bandstand. Clay knew it was important to her that everyone feel welcome and enjoy the celebration. They had a lot to celebrate, to be sure.

Mary Lou had initiated the work program, getting a lot of the open areas of the park plowed under and the areas set aside for planting large gardens. No one ate for free; everyone had to work in the community gardens.

Mary Lou had also set up hunting parties, and had even gone hunting as well. Clay had laughed at that. She was in for the long haul, ensuring they all had enough to eat. She was a good woman and worked hard along with everyone else.

The first few years had been hard, but Mary Lou had set up a seed swap at the celebration. Everyone was encouraged to share and swap seeds, also planting tips, and a thriving trade grew. Those living farther out came when they could, and there was always something to trade.

For Clay, there was very little work. Crime was nearly nonexistent. He worked alongside Mary Lou, hunting and working in the community garden. He also took food to outlying homes with elderly who couldn't make it. It was a community effort, but all benefited from it.

He and Katie were looking forward to seeing Harry and his group. It was nearly six months since they'd last seen them. Clay had received word that Steven had died several years ago. He was sad, but Gideon had come last year with Ginny and Robert, and they seemed fine.

The children were all growing up, and it amazed Clay how fast time was going. They'd all grown used to life without power, without computers and all the other things that had made life easier, yet more complicated.

They arrived at the park, and his boys ran off to join other children. He kept an eye on them, but there was little to worry about. He laughed when he saw Harry and walked over, embracing the other man.

"How the hell are you, Harry? Where are Marilyn and Willene?" Clay laughed.

"We're good. Marilyn is expecting this spring," he grinned.

"Congratulations! That is wonderful news! Katie will be tickled," he said, looking around for his wife, then spotting her. She'd already found

Willene and Marilyn, and they were all hugging each other.

He then saw Monroe and Earl. "My God, but Monroe has shot up over the summer. He's taller than his mother," Clay said, surprise on his face.

"Yeah. I think he'll be even taller than me," Harry laughed.

"I bet he's a big help," Clay said.

"He is. And Kimberly and Angela adore him. The girls follow him around, whether he wants it or not," Harry said and chuckled.

Boggy came up and shook Clay's hand, grinning.

"Hey, Boggy, how've you been?"

"Hey, Clay. Good. Been busy getting ready for winter," he laughed.

"Ain't that the truth," Earl said, coming up from behind.

Clay shook Earl's hand and smacked him on the back. Earl looked around, and grinned.

"Excuse me, boys. I think I done spotted the widow Baker," Earl said, and hurried off.

Clay laughed, and Harry shook his head.

"I think Earl is sweet on Erma Baker," Boggy laughed.

"I'd say you're right. She seems pretty taken with him too," Harry laughed.

"Looks like Boney and Bella May made it. Here they come," Clay said, pointing to a small carriage. Between the two was a teen. Bella May had taken in one of the many orphans and moved in with Boney to consolidate resources.

"Looks like Monroe isn't the only one getting tall, Jacob has grown at least six inches since I saw him last. I know he's a big help to Boney and Bella May," Clay said, watching as the small carriage pulled to the side, along with the other wagons and buggies.

Boggy turned and left the men, spotting a friend. Clay and Harry watched him leave, smiling. Then the two walked over to their wives.

The children played around them like wild puppies, their energy contagious as other children joined in. Laughter floated across the park, and people mingled and joined groups, then met with long-lost friends to catch up on gossip and memories.

Life had slowed down, but not stopped, in Beattyville. It was thriving, and though life was hard at times, it was good. There hadn't been any strangers, or any more conflicts. The survivors were few, but they were strong. They would continue.

Made in United States
North Haven, CT
26 November 2022